THE
MORBIDLY
OBESE
NINJA

Also by Carlton Mellick III

Satan Burger
Electric Jesus Corpse
Sunset With a Beard (stories)
Razor Wire Pubic Hair
Teeth and Tongue Landscape
The Steel Breakfast Era
The Baby Jesus Butt Plug
Fishy-fleshed
The Menstruating Mall
Ocean of Lard (with Kevin L. Donihe)
Punk Land
Sex and Death in Television Town
Sea of the Patchwork Cats
The Haunted Vagina
Cancer-cute (Avant Punk Army Exclusive)
War Slut
Sausagey Santa
Ugly Heaven, Beautiful Hell (with Jeffrey Thomas)
Adolf in Wonderland
Ultra Fuckers
Cybernetrix
The Egg Man
Apeshit
The Faggiest Vampire
The Cannibals of Candyland
Warrior Wolf Women of the Wasteland
The Kobold Wizard's Dildo of Enlightenment +2
Zombies and Shit
Crab Town

THE MORBIDLY OBESE NINJA

CARLTON MELLICK III

Eraserhead Press
Portland, OR

ERASERHEAD PRESS
205 NE BRYANT
PORTLAND, OR 97211

WWW.ERASERHEADPRESS.COM

ISBN: 1-936383-57-8

AUTHOR'S NOTE

So I've become a big anime nerd lately. Don't ask me how it happened. I think it started with the Samurai 7 anime, which I only watched because I'll watch anything Seven Samurai related. I was never into anime when I was younger, outside of a short period in high school when the novelty of cartoon sex was still appealing. But I watch anime all the time now. There's something about the plotting in anime that's really unique to that medium. You just don't see writing like it in American television, books, or movies. Unfortunately, the big drawback of becoming an anime nerd is that I have developed a fondness for J-pop and cute fluffy talking pink things. It's kind of creepy.

I wrote *Morbidly Obese Ninja* a few years ago, about the same time I wrote *Cybernetrix*. It was during a time when I was particularly obsessed with anime and thought it would be interesting to write a book set within an anime-like reality. So that's what I set out to do. This book was an experiment in creating anime in prose form. I won't be returning to the world of Morbidly Obese Ninja, but I will likely return to the style at some point in time.

Besides creating an anime novel, the other purpose of this book was to celebrate obesity. I think it's about time we acknowledge the awesomeness of the morbidly obese. It's not a medical condition. It's a super power.

So here it is. My 31st book release (I think). I hope you enjoy it. Tacos!

- Carlton Mellick III 4/13/2011 9:12 pm

ICHI

The ninja hadn't always been morbidly obese. He was once a firm, muscled warrior with the agility of a cat. But something happened to his eating habits that changed him. He started eating triple-triple cheeseburgers, glazed crème-filled donuts by the dozens, meat lovers deep-dish pizzas with garlic butter dipping sauce, goat cheese quesadillas wrapped around meatball sandwiches, chili-cheese tater tots topped with avocado egg rolls and ranch dressing, corndogs, candy bars, sausages, and mayonnaise. He ate everything with mayonnaise.

They called him Basu.

He was like a large black blimp overshadowing the moon as he dove from the sky onto the city of Neo Tokyo, California. His massive belly spilled out of his shinobi shozoku ninja outfit. Folds of fat rippled through the wind as he drew his iKatana from its scabbard and pointed it down at the rooftop of the Kakera Corporation building.

Five ninjas waited for him there. They jumped out from windows and from behind potted plants, swords in hand. They wore business suits beneath their black hoods, the Kakera company logo centered their ties.

Basu landed like a meteor, crushing a twenty-foot crater into the roof of the building. Two of the Kakera ninjas wavered in the impact, giving Basu an opening. His electronic katana left a blue trail of light as it sliced through their heads.

As the blood showered across the rooftop, the other three ninjas leapt into the air and flew at Basu from different directions. Basu deflected two of their attacks, then slammed them with his titanic belly, knocking them backward. His mass of flesh rumbled the building.

The third ninja struck him from behind, but Basu caught the blade between two rolls of fat. The ninja couldn't pull his sword free. Basu turned his head and glared at him. He shifted his weight, breaking the Kakera's iKatana in half, and then he split him down the middle. A geyser of blood sprayed into the moonlight.

Basu eyed the remaining two ninjas. He flipped through function modes on his iKatana, rolling the mouse ball on the handle with his thumb and right-clicking to get into information extraction mode.

The ninjas nodded at each other and then attacked. As Basu defended their strikes, his iKatana hacked into the CPUs of their swords, spider-crawling their databanks. The Kakeras attempted to hack Basu's iKatana as well, but they were unable to get past his iron-tight firewall.

As soon as he had sufficiently hacked each of the ninjas, Basu put all of his weight into a single attack. The Kakeras quickly switched their swords into full shield mode, but it was of no use to them. Even though they blocked his attack, Basu's blow was so powerful that it knocked them clear across the rooftop. Their bodies smashed into a brick wall.

One of them went limp and fell to the ground. The other hit the wall so hard he became embedded in the brick.

Blood streamed out of the Kakera's broken body as the obese ninja shuffled toward him. The wounded man tapped at a mini-keyboard on his iKatana, trying to relay information back to his boss via email, but before he could click *send* Basu's blade stabbed him through the heart. The morbidly obese ninja stared into his enemy's eyes as the life drained from him, and twisted the sword slowly between his ribs.

Before Basu gained all the weight, he was the deadliest corporate ninja in the electronics industry. After his weight went over 700 pounds, he also became the meanest.

Basu viewed the little screen on his iKatana and scrolled through the information he had retrieved from the dead ninjas.

Something wasn't right. Of the data he had extracted, there was very little information on the Kakera Corporation. Basu figured these security ninjas would at least have security codes and maps of the building, but there was no sign of data. In fact, Basu had more information on Kakera than these employees did.

After decrypting a couple of emails from their sent-box, Basu figured it out. He grunted as he leaned over a dead body and ripped a sleeve from its shoulder, revealing a tattoo of a smiley-faced teardrop. It was the Gomen company logo. These ninjas he had just killed were not employees of the Kakera Corporation. They were Gomen corporate ninjas in disguise.

Basu switched his iKatana to *camera mode* and took a digital photo of the tattoo. Then he went inside.

The top floor of the building was filled with dead bodies. There were twenty, perhaps thirty, dead Kakera ninjas littering the hallway. It was as if they had had their last stand here. Their iKatanas were all fried. The Kakeras probably knew they had no chance of winning and set the CPUs on their swords to *self-destruct mode* before their final battle began. Basu didn't see any Gomen corpses, so it must have been total annihilation.

Basu shifted his massive weight from side to side. He took three packets of mayonnaise out of a pouch on his uniform and squirted them through his thick crusty lips. As he rolled the white goop on his tongue, he put his iKatana on *phone mode* and called his employer at the Oekai corporate headquarters.

The phone picked up after one ring.

"Moshi moshi," said a raspy voice on the other end.

Basu swallowed the mayonnaise.

"We've got a problem," Basu said. His voice was deep and soft. He didn't speak very much, so his vocal cords were tender and smooth.

"Tell me," said his boss.

"The Gomen knew about the piggy bank," said Basu. "They beat me here."

There was a pause.

"Go after it," said his employer. There was no emotion to his tone at all. "This is a Class A mission. If you fail to retrieve the piggy bank you will be fired."

Fired was another word for executed.

Basu grunted into the phone. Then he turned it off.

Basu slid a small coin-sized disc from the bottom of the handle of his iKatana. The disc read *iPet*. When he turned it on, a plump green holographic frog appeared in his hand. It flicked its webbed feet and blinked its buggy eyes.

Kero-kero, croaked the cyber-frog.

Basu lifted the iPet to his face and frowned at it as if it were a fly that had landed on his cheeseburger. The cyber-frog stared back at Basu with a big cartoon smile.

Kero-kero, croaked the cyber-frog.

On the iKatana, Basu entered in the specs of the piggy bank, and then set the frog on the ground. The cyber-frog *kero-keroed*, spun around, and then hopped as fast as lightning down the hall.

Basu flew after it. He passed through blood-splattered hallways, hopping over several dead ninjas. All of the bodies were ninja. No other employees were in the building. It was against corporate ninja code to kill the daytime employees, which was why the ninjas worked night shift.

The cyber-frog hopped against walls and against the ceiling as it went. It hopped into a stairwell, and spiraled down twenty flights of stairs. Basu hopped after it, jumping down each flight, cracking the concrete under his heels every landing.

They soared across a sky bridge and went into the next building over. On the bridge, Basu looked over the edge, down into the abyss below. It stretched dozens of miles down. He could not see the bottom.

The next building was empty. There were no dead bodies here. This section of building belonged to a company that did not have a ninja staff, and therefore all employees had gone home for the evening.

The cyber-frog stopped in a wide-open lobby with gray plastic couches and kidney-shaped coffee tables. It hopped slowly up and down, waiting for Basu to retrieve it. As he sucked the holographic frog back into its disc, he saw a familiar face. He slid the disc into a pocket and squinted his eyes to be sure.

Across the room, through a glass wall, in a conference room, there was a man in a black suit surrounded by six Gomen ninjas.

The Gomen ninjas were not dressed like Kakeras. They were in their usual Gomen uniforms: brown leather shoes, a tan face mask, and a grayish-blue collared business-casual polo shirt tucked into khaki pants.

The man in the black suit stood taller than the others. He was as thin as a stickbug and had the head of a black bird.

He went by the name of Crow, but Basu knew him by his true name.

Cosmetic surgery had reached the point where humans could alter their appearance to look like anything their imaginations desired. People could change their genders with 100% accuracy, they could change their race, and they could change their age, even to that of a child's. Ten years ago, a trend popped up where people started getting cosmetic surgery to resemble animals. They altered their skin to look like snake scales, stretched their necks as long as those of giraffes, got extra limbs attached, and even got operations that turned them into actual swimming mermaids.

Crow had the operation to make himself look like a black bird. Although his entire body was human-shaped, he was covered in feathers. He had black beady eyes, a long hooked beak, and thin black claws at the ends of his fingers. Not a part of his operation, Crow also had a long scar running down the side of his face and through one of his eyes.

Basu and Crow had known each other for a long time. As he saw Crow blinking his black marble eyes, Basu wished he had permission to kill him. He squeezed his sausage fingers into a fist so hard the veins popped out of the back of his hand. There was nothing Basu wanted more on the planet than to kill this man, but it was something he could not do.

Two years ago, Crow had been promoted from ninja to an executive position in the Gomen Corporation. It was against ninja code to kill an executive of a company unless given explicit instructions from a CEO. No matter how much he wanted it, Basu could not kill Crow unless he was sent on an assassination mission explicitly calling for his head. Since there were fewer and fewer assassinations assigned, Basu had given up hope of ever getting a chance to kill him.

Crow was going to be a problem. When he was a ninja, he was the only man in the industry as deadly as Basu. But that was before Basu gained all the weight and before Crow became untouchable. Now, Crow would definitely have the upper hand in a fight.

Basu glared at his old rival. He watched his smug little crow head pacing the conference room, squawking at his men.

Crow dug his bird-like fingers into his suit and pulled out a small black sickle attached to a chain. He swung the sickle in a circle as he paced. Basu recognized the weapon. It was Crow's weapon of choice. When he was a ninja, he used to fight with it in addition to his iKatana. Basu could see that Crow no longer had a need for an iKatana, though. He had implanted an iPalm into his left hand, a common implant among executives.

After Basu's fingers eased out of his fist, he went in for a closer look.

Being morbidly obese made it difficult for Basu to use his stealth ability. He had to find shadows large enough to hide his size. The largest shadow in the room was only a few feet wide and only became thinner the closer it got to the conference room.

Only part of his body was concealed by shadow. His large round belly was sticking out in the light as he inched his way toward the conference room. The Gomen ninjas were too distracted by Crow's intimidating chain sickle to notice him, and Crow was too absorbed in his own squawking. That's what Basu was counting on. He hoped it would last.

Once he got a clear view of the conference room, Basu

scanned the area for the piggy bank. He was looking for something made of iron, something that was about seventy pounds.

There wasn't anything like that in the room. There was only Crow, his six ninjas, and the usual things one would find in a conference room. Basu examined more carefully. Then, as Crow paced away from the table, two new people came into view. There was another man in a suit. He had purple tentacles for hair and held a small device. There was also a little boy sitting next to him.

Basu wondered if the device the man held was the piggy bank. It was the size of a brick and had a small computer on its front. Then Basu realized what the device was. It wasn't the piggy bank. It was a mechanism for opening the piggy bank.

He watched what the tentacle man was doing with the device. He was putting it on the boy's chest, then taking it off of his chest and examining it, then typing on its keyboard.

Basu looked closer at the boy. He was about eight years old, wearing yellow shorts, tennis shoes, and a blue baseball cap. His Hawaiian shirt was pulled up and held in his teeth. The flesh underneath the boy's shirt was exposed. It wasn't flesh. It was iron. The boy was made of wrought iron. The little boy was the piggy bank.

Basu was close enough to turn the volume up on his iKatana so that he could hear inside of the conference room. He watched the man with the tentacles as he fidgeted desperately with the device.

"Is it ready yet?" squawked Crow, swinging the sickle over his head as though threatening the tentacled man with it.

"Almost," Tentacles said.

Basu could hear a ticking noise. It was coming from the boy. After a minute, the ticking began to slow.

"I need a wind-up," said the boy.

Tentacles slapped the boy across his cheek, then lowered his hand down to the metal section of his body and twisted the key on his hip until he was ticking at full pace again.

The boy sniffled. He did his best to stop himself from crying. His hands were tied behind his back. He wasn't able to wipe the tear of snot about to drip out of his nose.

"Okay," Tentacles said, smiling with razor teeth, "It's ready."

Crow put his sickle away.

"Good," he said. "Open him up."

Basu knew it was his only shot. He charged from the shadows and smashed through the glass wall of the conference room, then decapitated the tentacle-haired man before he got a chance to open the piggy bank.

Before the Gomen ninjas could react, Basu scooped up the machine boy and flew out of the room.

"What the . . ." Crow squawked, then he turned to his men, who had not even drawn their iKatanas yet. "Go after him!"

Basu flew through the building, the little boy dangling out of his flabby armpit. The boy stared up at him with wide eyes and a drooped open mouth.

Two ninjas quickly caught up to him, swinging their blades like reapers. Basu defended sloppily. Besides holding the boy, he was also preoccupied with trying to type an email on his iKatana. He needed to message for back up.

Before the email was sent, Basu's sword began to flicker. He looked down at it. The monitor on the handle was showing dozens of programs opening and closing at once, spamming up the CPU usage so much that he couldn't do anything with it.

Basu cursed the ninjas as he realized what they had done. Their iKatanas had been tipped with a computer virus that had broken through his firewall and infected his CPU. Basu stopped running and spun around, letting one of the ninjas charge right into his sword.

He wasn't able to get his weapon out of the dead ninja in time to defend against the other attacker's sword, so he caught the blade with his teeth and grabbed the ninja by the head. Basu's belly jiggled as he snapped the man's neck and tossed his corpse at the four ninjas flying toward him.

Basu turned and went for the elevator. He kicked a hole in the doors and then pried them open. Sweat as thick as engine grease oozed out of his flesh.

The machine boy raised his eyebrows as he looked over the edge. Then his blue cap fell off of his head and floated slowly down the elevator shaft. He couldn't see the bottom. It went hundreds of stories down.

Crow glided into the room like a locust and landed thirty feet away from Basu. His chain sickle spiraled in the air as he pitched it. The chain on the sickle stretched out of Crow's sleeve, making it all thirty feet to Basu.

But as the four ninjas arrived at the elevator, Basu

tossed one of them in front of the chain sickle. It hooked into the man's shoulder. As Crow pulled on the chain, the man flew backward like a fish being reeled out of the water. He went over Crow's shoulder, smashed through the window behind him, and dropped into the abyss.

Basu picked up the boy and jumped down the elevator shaft. He fell like a cannon ball, his sweat droplets raining upward into the boy's face.

On the way down, Basu grabbed the blue baseball cap, floating like a parachute in midair. Then he put it back on the boy's head and the boy smiled, patting the top of his hat.

After about thirty floors, he pushed off the side of the wall and crashed through an elevator door. He flew out of the building, across another sky bridge, through a few more buildings and a few more sky bridges. Then they arrived in a crowded mall.

The mall was old world. It was a large open room lined with rows and rows of vendors selling over-salted meats and curly vegetables. The people walked like zombies from booth to booth, buying random trinkets and bottles of soup.

The machine boy grinned as Basu carried him through the mall like a football.

Basu looked down and wondered what the heck the boy was smiling at. He frowned at him in the same way he frowned at the cyber-frog. Then he grunted.

"You're huge!" cried the boy, looking up at Basu with wide amazed eyes.

Basu grunted.

"You're like the size of a bus!" said the boy.

Basu squeezed him tightly in his armpit for saying that, but the squeezing only hurt Basu. The iron boy didn't feel a thing.

"That's why they call me Basu," he said. "It means *bus*."

"Oh," said the boy, flicking the brim of his hat. "They call me Oki."

Crow and his remaining men entered the mall. Basu wasn't surprised they were able to catch up with him. Crow was nearly impossible to escape. Basu knew he had to use a new trick, since Crow knew all of his old ones.

Basu squeezed into a small space between booths. He squished the boy into his belly and climbed backward up the wall. His black outfit spread out until he looked like a black tarp connecting the two booths on his sides.

Crow and his men split up and scanned the mall. One of the ninjas came up to the booth next to Basu, but he was looking behind the counter of the booth rather than above, as if he suspected the frizzy-haired vendor might have been hiding them. As the ninja stepped by, the machine boy started squirming against Basu's gut. The sweat dripping onto the back of the boy's neck was tickling him, making him giggle.

Basu flexed his arms to hold the boy still and squeezed his breasts together to muffle his giggles. He hoped that the sound of the crowd was enough to cover up the sounds of the boy's ticking mechanical body.

The ninja didn't notice. He lost interest and went back to the others.

NI

Basu waited up there for another forty minutes. He wasn't sure if Crow had left or if he had just pretended to leave and was really just waiting for Basu to come out of hiding. After forty minutes of holding the wiggling machine boy against his belly, Basu figured it was safe to get down. Once they were on the ground, the boy stretched and then wound himself up.

"You're greasy," said the boy, drawing a smiley face in the sweat of a love handle sticking out of Basu's suit.

Basu grunted and swatted his finger away. Then he removed his hood and pushed a button on the neck of his shinobi shozoku ninja outfit. The ninja suit brightened and its colors transformed to appear as if he were wearing blue jeans and a white shirt. Even though Crow knew his true appearance, he figured he would have an easier time escaping the Gomen ninja if he blended in with the common citizens.

He took the boy by the hand and walked him to a food cart that sold salami and sauerkraut tacos. He barged through the line, knocking furry-fleshed men and fish-eyed women out of the way. The other citizens didn't stop him. Even though his ninja suit had been transformed, they could tell by his iKatana that he was ninja.

The wrinkled bearded man at the stand was amazed at how many tacos Basu ordered. He ordered more than the man had. Basu ate the tacos as quickly as the man could make them. He squeezed mayonnaise from his pocket onto every bite.

Oki stared up at the obese ninja with amazement as he watched him snort and grunt and swallow tacos whole.

"Bus!" said the boy, tugging on his uniform. "Stop."

Basu looked down at the boy with one eye as he gorged on the food.

"You can't eat so much," said the boy.

The vendor tossed up two more tacos and Basu folded them together and stuffed them into his mouth.

"Why?" Basu said with a full mouth, hairs of sauerkraut dangling over his lips.

"If you eat so much there won't be enough for anyone else," Oki said, pointing to the long line of people behind them.

Basu gave the other people in line a glance. They stepped back a little. Then Basu went back to eating.

"I have to eat," said the ninja.

"But why?" said the boy. "No one eats that much."

"It's important."

Basu had to consume at least 45,000 calories every day. If he didn't he would die. Three years ago he was stabbed with an iKatana that was laced with a nano-poison. The poison was completely impossible to extract once it got under the skin. Those poisoned with it would die in less than 48 hours after it hit the bloodstream. The only way to keep the poison from spreading was to consume 45,000 calories or more per day. The excess calories stunned the nanobots, and kept them from eating apart his body from the inside out.

Although the poison could be survived this way, it was still widely used amongst corporate ninjas, because very few people were able to keep up with consuming 45,000 calories every day. And those who were able to eat so much food quickly became bedridden. They could no longer work and had to be taken care of by family members for the rest of their lives.

Basu was the first ninja infected with the poison to ever continue working as a ninja. He exercised twice as hard every day to be able to move around his mass of flesh. He figured out ways to make his weight work for him as a ninja, rather than slow him down.

He had to spend a lot of his day eating, but he grew to love the taste of greasy foods. He had had such a strict diet for most of his life, and now he was finally given a chance to indulge himself. The best part was that his company paid for everything he ate, so he could buy whatever his heart desired, as long as it was high in calories.

There were times when Basu thought the nano-poison was the best thing that ever happened to him. But, other times, when his heart felt like a lump of rusted metal in his chest, he wished the poison would just finish him off and put him out of his misery.

After the taco cart was out of food, the other customers slinked away from the line. Oki saw their frowning faces and tugged on Basu's uniform.

"Look," said the boy. "You made them all sad."

Basu grunted and walked the boy out of the mall. They went a few buildings down and then took an elevator up to a rooftop.

"Where are we going?" Oki said.

"I need to get you back to my company." Basu looked down at his iKatana. The screen was frozen. He couldn't even get it to reboot. "But we can't go back until I get my sword cleaned of this virus."

"Oh," said the boy.

Then the boy said, "Why not?"

"The Gomen will be waiting for us if we go back to my company." Basu licked taco grease from the back of his hand. "They know who I work for."

"Oh," said the boy, nodding his head.

Then the boy said, "So where are we going?"

"I know someone who can help," Basu said. "She's the only programmer I know who I can trust right now."

"Oh," said the boy.

Then the boy said, "Who is she?"

"I'm not talking anymore," Basu said. "You make my throat hurt."

They went to the Japanese side of town. Basu didn't know why they called it the Japanese side of town, since over 90% of the city was Japanese. Many of the Japanese people spread through the city weren't born Japanese, though. A lot of people got cosmetic surgery to look Japanese. It was a popular racial trend. Everyone wanted to be Japanese to fit in. Nobody could tell the true Japanese from the modified Japanese, because the operations were so accurate and everyone was taught to speak fluent Japanese as children.

The second most common race was a completely new race of human. They were called *animese*, which were people who got cosmetic surgery to look like anime characters.

As they walked into a plaza of hover shops that floated in the space between four apartment buildings, Oki saw dozens of these anime-made-flesh people. They all had unrealistic curves and looked lighter than air. Their eyes were huge ovals and their mouths were tiny dots. Their flesh looked bleached of all color and texture.

Some of the more traditional people were prejudiced against the animese. A hateful term for animese was *bug-eye*, because one undesirable effect of getting eye-enlargement surgery was that it caused the front of your eyeballs to hang nearly an inch out of the sockets.

Oki had never seen anything like them before. He held Basu's hand tightly as they passed a trio of anime girls. When the girls laughed, their giant eyes became thin slits and their tiny mouths turned into giant gaping holes that took up most of their faces. Their laughing faces made Oki shiver and hide behind the mammoth ninja.

Basu took him to a shop on the edge of the hovering plaza. The shop had a sign that read, *Hollow World*. Hollow was a cutesy way of spelling *holo*, as in holographic video games. There was another sign that read, *closed*.

"No one's here, Bus," Oki said.

"She's here," Basu said.

After a few minutes of knocking, the door opened. Oki scooted behind Basu's knees as he saw who was at the door. It was another anime girl. She had bright pink hair, and a white schoolgirl uniform with a blue skirt hiked up so high you could see part of her Hello Kitty panties. Unlike most of animese women, her breasts weren't actually bigger than her head.

She took a long look at Basu.

"Chiya," Basu said.

"Basu," the woman said.

They glared at each other for a few minutes.

Then the woman burst into the giggles of a hyperactive teenager.

"Basu-Basu!" she cried, and then sprang into the air and landed on his chest.

She wrapped her arms around his neck, her legs around his back, kissing his chubby forehead and bouncing her cartoonish butt on top of his belly.

25

"Where have you been?" she cried with a wide-open mouth.

Basu grunted.

Then the anime woman saw Oki hiding behind him.

"Oh, wow!" she said, jumping off of Basu's stomach and approaching the boy.

"Hi, there!" she said. "I'm Chiya Takahashi! It's the greatest pleasure to meet you!"

Then she cocked her head to the side and gave him a kawaii peace sign.

"I'm Oki," said the boy, and then buried his eyes in Basu's hip.

"I'm sure we're going to be the greatest of friends!" she said.

Then she scrambled them into her shop and closed the door.

Hollow World was a game shop as a front. Chiya made most of her money when the shop was closed. She was a specialist in creating programs for iKatanas and other computerized weaponry. Besides being a shop, Hollow World was also Chiya's personal hover-bus and apartment.

Once inside, Basu handed Chiya his sword.

"It's been hit with a nasty virus," Basu said. "I think it's something new."

"Hmmm . . ." Chiya examined the sword. "I doubt it. How many days do I got?"

"I need it right now," Basu said.

"Of course," Chiya said.

She put the iKatana on a desk littered with tiny computers and purple teddybears dressed in little homemade leather bondage outfits. Then she noticed Oki was shaking.

"Whoa," she said with her mouth drooping to the bottom right corner of her face. "What's wrong, little guy?"

Oki wouldn't speak.

"He's frightened," Basu said. "He's never seen an animese woman before."

The anime woman laughed with gyrating shoulders. "Where the heck has he been?"

"He's had a sheltered life," Basu said.

Then he lifted the child's shirt to reveal his wrought iron body.

Chiya leaned in for a closer look.

"Oh!" she said. "A live piggy bank! Wow! I've never seen one before."

"What is he, exactly?" Basu said. "My boss never told me I was to retrieve a child."

"He probably didn't know," she said, talking out of the side of her mouth with one raised eyebrow. "Piggy banks are rarely children."

Chiya looked down and examined the boy's body. Oki shuddered as she wiped her finger along his neck to where his flesh met with metal. Then she squeezed his arms and legs, feeling where his body connected with the machine. His entire torso was metal. His limbs and head were flesh. He didn't have any sexual organs. Then her finger went to his hip. She grabbed his key and wound him up.

As she listened to the ticking in his chest, she said, "They use piggy banks to save important information.

27

They are mechanical rather than electronic so that it is completely impossible to hack into them and retrieve the information. If you try to break into them by force the information is destroyed."

Basu grunted.

She looked over at him, her pupils widening across the whites of her eyes. "And the reason they call them piggy banks is because you can only open them once."

"Once?" Basu said.

"You can put as much data as you want inside," she said. "But to retrieve the information you have to break the bank that holds it."

Basu frowned at the mechanical boy.

"I see," Basu said. "If he is opened then he will die."

"Correctomundo," she said, winking her giant eye at the mechanical boy.

Basu frowned and then grunted.

Oki pulled his shirt down over his metal chest and stepped away from the animese girl.

Basu was quite familiar with the Kakera Corporation. He knew they were something of an anomaly in the industry. Instead of putting most of their money into hiring the best ninja, they put their money into research. With a weak defense and a wealth of secrets, the Kakera Corporation made a prime target for the ninjas of other electronics companies. Especially for companies such as Gomen, who put all their money into ninjas and weaponry instead of research, relying solely on stealing the technology of their competitors.

The anomaly of Kakera was that they have used their research to create new ways of keeping their information safe. They learned early on that a strong ninja defense was never strong enough. So they began inventing technologies, such as the piggy banks, that would protect their information even if it fell into the wrong hands.

Oki was the ultimate piggy bank. In order to steal the information, a competitor would have to murder a child. Very few companies were cut-throat enough to kill children in order to steal secrets.

Although Basu had not known that the piggy bank was going to be a young boy, he had known that it possessed an incredible wealth of information. It contained all of the new products that Kakera planned to put into development, but did not yet have the funds to move forward with. This was the curse of Kakera. They had brilliant ideas for products, but never had enough funding to move their projects forward. It would take a bigger company, such as Gomen or Oekai, to make them work.

Oekai and Gomen were the two largest companies in the industry. Whichever one ended up with the piggy bank would get so far ahead in the game that it would bury the other in less than a year. Basu knew the Gomen were going to do whatever it took to get the piggy bank back.

SAN

Chiya got right to work on his iKatana. For safety purposes, Chiya put her store into hover-bus mode and detached from the plaza. She wanted to stay on the move to make it harder for the Gomen to find them. Basu agreed it was a good idea. Her plan was to move the bus once an hour to a different side of town.

While Chiya worked, she gave Basu access to her kitchen and he made full use of it. He pulled every bit of meat she had out of the freezer: three packages of bacon, six tubes of sausage, a bag of meatballs, and some ahi tuna steaks. He fried them all up in the same skillet, draining the grease into a coffee can that he put in the refrigerator.

Basu wasn't sure why Chiya had so much meat in her freezer. She wasn't much of a carnivore. It looked like it had been there for a long time, as if she had kept it in there just in case he came back.

On the two-seat dining table, Basu shoveled the greasy meats into his mouth from a serving platter. He had a fork in each hand. Oki sat across from him, watching with bemusement. The machine boy leaned forward in his chair with his chin in his hands, hanging on the ninja's every movement.

"How do you fit it all in?" Oki asked.

Basu grunted at him with a full mouth of chewed sausage.

Oki's stomach started to growl within his metal torso. He touched his cold hard belly.

"Can I have some?" Oki asked.

Basu stared up at him. He chewed for a while and then swallowed.

"Do you even need to eat?" Basu asked.

The boy nodded. "Of course I do."

Basu angrily stabbed down on his mountain of meat with a fork, splattering grease across the table like a small bomb had just gone off. The boy sat up straight in his chair, wondering what he had done wrong. Basu pulled his fork out of the pile. There was a meatball on the end of it. He handed the fork to Oki and then went right back to shoveling food into his mouth. With one fork missing, he used his bare hand to pick up sausages and squeeze them into the side of his mouth as he chewed.

Oki smiled at the meatball on the fork. He twisted it around in his hand, spinning it in circles as he nibbled around the edges.

After Basu had finished eating, he took the meat grease out of the fridge. It had congealed into a white paste that he scooped out with a butter knife and spread on four slices of toast. He added cinnamon and sugar and called it dessert.

After dinner, Oki and Basu sat on the couch together. Oki looked up at Basu. The size of Basu never ceased to amaze the boy.

"What's that for?" Oki asked, pointing at a hover-scooter in the corner of the room.

Basu grunted.

Oki kept staring at him, waiting for an answer.

"It's for flying," Basu said.

"Is it fun?" Oki asked.

Basu grunted.

They stared at the floor for a while.

"So what do you do for fun?" Oki asked. "Besides fighting and eating."

Basu grunted.

"Do you have any roboplex dolls?"

Basu grunted.

"What about turbo balls?"

Basu grunted.

"Holo-cards?"

Basu let out a long grunt. Then a short one.

"You know what your problem is?" Oki said. "You don't know how to have fun."

Basu looked at him.

Oki pointed at his metal chest. "I try to have at least a little bit of fun every single day. You should try it. If you had more fun things to do maybe you wouldn't eat so much."

They sat in silence for a few minutes. Basu looked around the room. Then he pulled the iPet disc out of his pocket and turned it on. The cartoon cyber-frog caught Oki's attention as it popped up into the air and landed on Basu's lap.

The plump cyber-frog looked at Oki with a big cartoon smile. It hopped up into the air and did a flip for him. Oki moved closer. The frog flipped again. Then again. It smiled every time it flipped.

Oki looked up at the obese man.

Basu winked at him. Then he looked down at the flipping frog, then back at Oki, and back at the frog. Then Basu smiled and grunted a little laugh.

"What?" Oki said.

Basu grunted and looked down at the frog. Then grunted a louder laugh.

"What?" Oki repeated. "Is that supposed to be fun or something?"

Basu stopped smiling.

Oki laughed. "That is the dumbest toy I've ever seen. Look at it."

Oki pointed at the frog as it smiled and hopped.

"That toy's for babies!" Oki said.

Oki burst into more laughter, pointing at Basu.

Basu frowned.

"You play with a baby toy!" Oki teased.

Then Basu grunted angrily. He snatched the cyber-frog out of the air, flicked it off, and put the disc back into his pocket. Then he jumped off of the couch and stomped out of the room, while Oki lay on his back kicking his feet up in the air with laughter.

Basu ran into Chiya in the kitchen.

"I need to get some sleep," she said, rubbing her swollen eyelids.

She yawned so wide her mouth became the size of a dinner plate.

"Is it done?" he asked.

"Not yet," she said. "You'll have to spend the night. I'll finish in the morning."

"I needed it done by now," he said. "Oekai is expecting me back tonight."

"You're not getting it done tonight," she said.

Basu sighed. He didn't feel comfortable out on the streets without a functioning CPU on his iKatana.

"Okay," Basu said.

She stepped away from him and went to the counter to pour herself some sake.

Basu looked out of the hover-bus window, examining the vast landscape of lights and buildings. He knew that Crow was out there somewhere, looking for him. He knew that before this mission was over, he was going to have to face him again.

Crow and Basu had known each other for years, back when they went by their real names, before Crow became birdlike and Basu became morbidly obese. Crow's name was Susumu. Basu's name was Keigo.

They went through training together and both graduated at the top of their class. Both were recruited by the same company, Arashi Industries. They moved up the ranks together. They became Arashi Industries's star employees and each became a general of his own small army. They wore the burgundy-red suits and red ties that were the signature uniform of the Arashi. They wore the white five-horned masks of the Arashi ninja.

Although they thought of themselves as equals, Keigo was considered the company's champion and Susumu was considered his understudy.

Keigo was stronger and a little faster with a sword, but Susumu was smarter, cleverer, and quicker at working the computer functions on his iKatana, not to mention that he was proficiently ambidextrous and could fight with a chain sickle in his left hand while swinging a sword with his right. Susumu also had twice the number of kills over Keigo. But Keigo was still regarded as the deadliest ninja in the industry.

Susumu resented the fact that his talents were not fully recognized by his employer. He resented Keigo for making more money. In time, Susumu grew tired of Arashi Industries, and eventually he grew tired of his friend Keigo.

Their friendship ended the day Susumu became Crow. After a couple years in Keigo's shadow, Susumu decided to show the world he was the industry's true champion ninja. He broke his sworn oath to stay forever loyal to Arashi Industries. He sold company secrets to the Gomen Corporation and helped with a hostile takeover that resulted in the largest company war of the decade. One day, Keigo walked into a meeting and discovered the conference room filled with headless executives. They were sitting around the table in their red suits and red ties, their posture straight and alert, their hands folded neatly in front of them. But their heads weren't attached to their necks. They were on the table in front of them, staring at each other with blank eyes.

Aside from the dead executives, there were three men standing in the room. Two were Gomen in business-casual ninja outfits. The third was a man with a crow head wearing the Arashi Industries red suit and tie.

Keigo raised his iKatana and pointed it at the black-feathered man.

"I'm so happy you could get here on time, Keigo," said the crow man.

Keigo took off his mask. "How do you know who I am?"

The crow man cocked his head and pointed the handle of his iKatana at him. "Everybody knows the great Keigo of the Arashi."

Keigo lifted his sword, ready to strike at any second. "Who are you? Why do you disgrace the Arashi by wearing that uniform?"

The crow man hopped up onto the conference table and clicked across with his black bird feet.

"You think you're so strong, don't you, Keigo?" said the crow man. "But you're not the best. You've just made everybody think you're the best."

The crow pulled a black chained-sickle out of his suit. Keigo recognized the weapon. He looked up at the crow man. Then he recognized the suit he was wearing. He recognized a tone in the crow's voice.

"Susumu?" Keigo said.

The crow paused. It was as if he was smiling, but no smile could be seen with a beak on his face.

Then the crow attacked. Clinking metal sounds ripped through the air as the chain sickle flew at Keigo. Jumping two feet back, Keigo knocked the sickle out of the air with his iKatana.

"Susumu was a fool," said the crow. "He no longer exists. I am Crow."

Crow struck again with his sword. Keigo dodged. The sword sliced less than an inch away from his throat.

"Susumu," Keigo said, dodging the attacks. "What have you done to our executives?"

The sickle was reeled back toward Crow's black claw fingers, cutting into Keigo's shoulder.

"They were fools, too, Keigo," said Crow. "It is shameful to be a fool. I put them out of their misery."

The two Gomen ninja joined the fight, forcing Keigo to defend against all three men, but Keigo would not yet take the offensive.

"Susumu, you are my closest friend," Keigo said. "What have you done?"

Crow twirled his sickle like a helicopter blade, holding it in front of him as if using it as a shield.

"What have *I* done?" said Crow. "What have *you* done? I'm not the one responsible for turning these men into fools. It was you. You made them believe that you were the strongest ninja in the industry when we both know that you are not. You have disgraced yourself and Arashi Industries. Neither of you should be allowed to live."

Keigo composed himself. "I see. You could no longer advance with me in your way. I understand."

Then Keigo sliced the sword-arm off of one of the Gomen. Blood exploded onto Keigo's red suit. The Gomen stood there, shrieking in agony, staring at the red fluid geysering out of his stump across the conference table.

"If killing me is the only way you can prove your honor," Keigo said, "then I must not deny you this fight. As my closest friend, I owe you this much."

Crow's sickle stopped twirling and shot out of his hand at Keigo, wrapping around his sword arm.

"Fuck honor," Crow said. "This is about revenge."

Crow yanked on Keigo's arm and pulled him closer. As Keigo was reeled into range, Crow swung his iKatana and carved a wedge of meat out of Keigo's thigh. Blood mixed with his burgundy uniform.

Keigo cried out and slashed at Crow with his iKatana, but Crow's new body was faster than his old one. The sword passed over his feathered head and decapitated the screaming armless ninja beside him.

Crow back-flipped onto the conference table and swept the room with his chain sickle. Keigo ducked, but the other Gomen ninja coming up behind him was not fast enough. The chain wrapped around the ninja's neck three times and then the sickle stabbed into his throat. The Gomen wheezed and drooled blood, struggling to free himself from the metal noose.

Keigo took the opportunity to lunge at Crow. He jumped up on the table and slashed at Crow's chest. The red suit ripped open and black feathers spilled into the air. Crow's red tie dropped to the ground. The front of his suit slid off like a slice of cheese.

"You don't deserve to wear that uniform," Keigo said.

"It doesn't matter. I'm Gomen now."

With that, Crow yanked on his chain sickle, ripping the Gomen ninja's head from his neck. Keigo dodged the severed head at the end of the sickle as it swung toward him, giving Crow a chance to click his iKatana into *nano-poison mode*.

The head fell off the sickle and rolled down the table. Keigo saw an opening. He hacked down on the chain of Crow's signature weapon in an attempt to render it useless. But Crow managed to spin the chain, wrapping Keigo's iKatana, disabling Keigo's weapon instead. Then Crow stabbed Keigo through the belly with his sword.

Keigo fell to his knees.

"It's the end," Crow said.

Crow stepped away from his ex-friend as blood leaked out of his body and tiny nanobots began spreading through his bloodstream.

Keigo could feel the poison. It was a sparkling sensation that crawled through his wound and up his spine.

"You and Arashi Industries are a thing of the past," Crow said, hopping off of the conference table and turning on a wall monitor.

The monitor displayed a scene of the Arashi lobby. Two dozen ninjas in red suits were battling perhaps a hundred Gomen ninjas. The Arashi were falling quickly. They fought in three inches of blood.

Crow went back to Keigo. "I wanted you to see this. Those are your men dying out there. All of the Arashi men who were loyal to me are now in Gomen uniforms, fighting against the Arashi."

Keigo tried to build up his strength, just enough strength to swing his sword one last time. If he could defeat Crow he would be able to die with honor. But his strength wasn't coming back to him. He lay on his stomach, holding his iKatana tightly beneath him.

Crow made him watch as the Gomen defeated his men. He waited until every last one of them was dead. Then he turned the monitor off. He went to Keigo.

"It's too bad it happened this way," Keigo said, then coughed up a line of blood. "You were my closest friend. I wish circumstances never would have led you on such a dishonorable path."

Crow lifted his sword.

"Honorable or dishonorable," he said. "It's still progress."

Then Crow swung his sword. Keigo push-upped off of the conference table, elevating his body three feet off the surface. Crow's sword missed and gave Keigo an opening.

Keigo's iKatana swung out to his side, slicing across the right side of Crow's face. It cut through his feathered cheek, through his forehead, through his beady black eye.

Crow screeched and stepped back. Keigo ran. He didn't have the strength to fight anymore. He just ran. He had the nano-poison running through his veins and he knew the only way he could survive was to eat. He had to eat as much high-calorie food as he possibly could.

SHI

Basu thrashed himself awake, clutching his chest. He threw off the sweat-stained covers and sat up on the edge of the octagon-shaped bed. He leaned over and took deep breaths, holding his heart to make sure it was still beating.

Chiya sat up behind him and wrapped her arms around his neck. She pressed her naked breasts against his sweaty back and leaned her cheek on his shoulder.

"You're still having your attacks," she said.

Basu took a few more deep breaths before answering. "It's just sleep apnea," he said.

She rubbed her fingers through his hair and down the folds on the back of his neck.

"That's what you always used to say," she said, her voice like a hum against his left ear.

Basu closed his eyes and fell backward in the bed, breaking free of her embrace.

The anime woman laid her head on his chest and listened to his heart. "You can't keep going like this. It's going to kill you."

He placed his baseball-mitt-sized hand onto her back. "You know I'll die if I stop."

"You just need to eat less cholesterol," she said. "Eat more sugars. Cut out the saturated fats. Try eating foods with omega-3 fatty acids like salmon and tuna. I have some ahi tuna steaks in the freezer if you want some."

"I already ate them," he said.

"Yeah, with bacon and sausage . . ." she said.

Basu let out a long sigh.

"You used to be so sexy," she said, rubbing the hairs on his chest. "I wish you didn't make me call you Basu."

"That's who I am now," he said.

"I'm still working on a way to extract the nanos," she said.

"Don't bother," he said. "I'll be long dead before you can figure that one out."

"I'll do it," she said. "You know I will."

Her tone of voice told him she didn't even believe the words herself.

Basu grunted.

"Why don't you stay with me?" she said. "For good this time."

Basu slid his arm off of her back. She lifted her head from his chest and looked at him inches away from his face, eye to enormous eye.

"That piggy bank we got there in the other room has to be worth a fortune," she said. "We can sell it and retire. We can move to Hawaii or somewhere in the Caribbean. I'll figure out how to extract the nanos and you'll get thin again. We'll live in paradise, just you and me."

Basu pushed her off of him and stepped out of the bed. Then he pulled his pants on.

She blinked her wide eyes at him.

"I can't just sell him," Basu said.

"Why not?" she said, her eyebrows curled and her mouth stretched wider across her face. "He's going to die anyway, no matter which company ends up with him."

"I'm sorry," he said. "It would go against the ninja

code. *My* code."

"Screw your fucking code," she said, throwing a pillow into his face and pulling the covers over her head like a 5-year-old.

Basu put his shirt on and went into the other room. Oki wasn't asleep on the couch where they had left him. The blanket was on the floor. The front door of the shop was wide open.

The bus hovered in open space between two buildings, so Oki could not have run away. Basu walked through the front door out onto the porch. Oki was sitting on the edge, staring down at the abyss below.

Basu sat next to him. His weight rocked the bus back and forth as he plopped down. He put his finger up to Oki's cheek and wiped a tear away.

"You heard us?" Basu said.

The machine boy nodded his head, still glaring down into the abyss. Basu was surprised he had been able to hear them. He wondered if the Kakera Corporation supplied the boy with superior hearing, perhaps so he could hear danger when it was coming his way.

"She wants to kill me," Oki said in a croaky voice.

Basu grunted. "I won't let her."

"You want to kill me, too," the boy said.

Basu looked away.

"I don't want to kill you," he said. "But I don't have a choice. It's my duty."

Oki's watery eyes shivered at Basu. "But why? Why is your duty so important?"

Basu slapped Oki across the cheek.

Oki jerked with shock, then trembled beneath the ninja's fat angry face.

"Have some dignity," Basu said to the scared little boy. "Just as my role in life is to follow my company's orders without question, it is your role in life to be a piggy bank. You were born to hold information and you will die once that information is needed. Accept your fate. It is the honorable thing to do."

Oki took a breath and wiped tears from his eyes. Basu stared down into the abyss below, watching his plump feet dangling in space.

"It's a long away down, isn't it?" Basu said.

Oki nodded.

"What's down there?" Oki asked, his eyes still tearing.

"Miles down are the old streets," he said. "We don't use them anymore, except for waste disposal. You can still see the streets in smaller towns, outside of California, where buildings are far apart and only thirty stories tall."

"Thirty stories tall?" Oki laughed through his tears. "You're making fun of me."

"No," Basu chuckled. "There are many buildings out there that are even shorter than that."

Oki smiles. "I wish I could be on a building less than thirty stories high."

"Why?" Basu said.

"So I could see the ground," Oki said.

"There's nothing great about seeing the ground," Basu said.

"I don't know," Oki said. "I've never seen it before."

Basu looked down into the abyss. After a hundred stories, all he could see was a single point. The ground was farther down than his eyes could see.

"There are a lot of things I've never seen," Oki said.

Basu didn't know what to say to him. He lifted his arm to put it around Oki's back, but changed his mind at the last second and leaned it against the post that held up the green canopy over the shop.

"Bus?" Oki said.

Basu grunted.

"If I have to die," Oki said. "Can you make sure that I get to see the ground first?"

Basu grunted.

The boy smiled up at the giant ninja and leaned against his shoulder. Basu looked down at him and patted him awkwardly on the head. He noticed that the boy's ticking was beginning to slow, so he wound him up as far as he could.

GO

In the morning, Basu awoke on the floor next to the couch with a tiny blanket on his stomach that might as well have been the size of a washcloth. Oki was not on the couch next to him.

Basu went into the storefront section of the hover-bus, but it was empty apart from the shelves of holo-games. In the front of the hover-bus, he found Chiya driving. She was steering between buildings, circling.

"What's going on?" Basu asked. "Where's Oki?"

Chiya looked over at him and blinked her cartoon eyes slowly. Then turned back. "Probably asleep."

"In the bedroom?" Basu asked. "He wasn't on the couch."

Chiya shrugged, driving the bus slowly through the open space between companies. Basu looked out of a window. He could see people inside of the buildings, eating cereal, kissing each other on the cheek, chatting with their children. It was the life of the daytime employees. It was a life that Basu, Chiya, and Oki would never know.

"Is my sword ready yet?" Basu asked.

Chiya shook her head. "Not yet."

"Why aren't you working on it?" he asked.

"Looking for a good spot to park," she said.

She drove the bus in circles. There were plenty of places for her to park.

"You're stalling," Basu said.

Chiya giggled. "What?"

Basu grunted.

Then he said, "You're not finishing my sword on purpose. You think you might be able to convince me to sell the boy and run away with you if you had some extra time."

"That's ridiculous," Chiya said, rubbing her fingers against the sweaty steering wheel. "I am a professional."

She looked at Basu with her wide black pupils and then looked back at the sky.

Basu squinted at her. He saw something in that look. Something he hadn't seen before.

"Wait a minute . . ." Basu said. "You're stalling for another reason, aren't you?"

Chiya didn't say anything. She relaxed her shoulders. Basu knew he was right.

"You sold us out," he said. "How could you of all people sell me out?"

"Look . . ." She exhaled with mock irritation, then looked at him with slits for eyes. "I wasn't selling *you* out. I just wanted to sell the piggy bank, so that we would have enough money to run away together."

"Who did you call?" he said.

"I know that you want to be with me," she said. "If I can just get you away from your job, this city, I know you'll be happier."

Basu slammed his fist into the side window and it shattered into a spiderweb of cracks.

"*Who* did you call?" he said.

"Gomen," she said.

"What?" he cried, shoving his face into hers.

47

"They're the biggest company," she said. "I knew they'd pay the most money for it."

Basu yelled out until his voice became scratchy and raw. Then he turned away from her, rocking the bus back and forth.

He said, "You stupid, stupid bug-eye."

"Don't call me bug-eye, fatass!" she said.

"You think they're actually going to pay you?" he said in a raspy voice. "They'll kill you without a second thought."

"But I did it for you," she said.

"Why?" he said. "Why do anything for me? You're my emergency katana programmer that I occasionally sleep with. We mean nothing to each other."

"I love you," she cried.

"Big fucking deal," he said.

As Basu turned to leave the room, Chiya jumped from the driver's seat and charged him. She pulled a switchblade out of her boot and drove it into his hip.

"What do you mean *big fucking deal?*" she shrieked into his ear.

She wrapped her arm around his neck, squeezed her legs around his back, and stabbed him again in the chubby shoulder. Basu thrashed as if he had a spider crawling on him. His baggy arms couldn't reach her.

With no one at the wheel, the bus spun out of control. It ground against the side of a building, heading in a downward slope.

"I've been waiting years for you," she said, piercing the blade through a fold of fat on his neck. "You promised me."

Basu grunted at her. "When?"

"When you were Keigo," she said.

He jerked forward and slammed her into the wall headfirst. She hit it with a clunk and fell to the floor.

"I'm not Keigo anymore," he said.

Basu took control of the hover-bus, and pulled it to a stop on the side of a sky bridge. He held the wound on his hip, his blood trailing across the carpet as he staggered through the bus to make sure Oki was okay. He went into the bedroom. It was empty. He went upstairs into the loft. It was empty. The storefront was empty.

He noticed that the front door was open. He went out onto the porch. It was crushed in on itself, ripped apart when the bus had collided with the building. The boy wasn't there. He hoped Oki hadn't been out there when the bus went out of control.

When he went back inside, he noticed that the hover-scooter was missing. The boy must have escaped.

"Chiya, you bitch," he said.

He took the iKatana off of Chiya's desk and turned it on. It seemed to be working fine. He wondered if she had finished it last night but pretended it still needed work.

Basu left red footprints as he staggered back to the front of the bus. Chiya was regaining consciousness, rubbing the top of her head. Basu picked her up by the elbow and tossed her out of the cockpit into the storefront area. Then he closed the door.

He couldn't fit his massive weight into the driver's seat,

49

so he ripped it out and tossed it through the window. Then he squatted down and drove off, back to the area where Chiya had been circling.

He pulled some mayonnaise packets out of his pants and squirted them into his mouth. Then sucked down four more packets. Then four more. The white goo mixed with the red blood on his fingers. Pink globules rolled down his chin, splattering his belly like bird shit.

Basu grunted. He pulled his iPet disc out of his pocket and it flipped on. The plump cyber-frog sat in his hand with languid eyes, as if it were half-asleep.

Kero-kero, it croaked, as if asking *what the hell do you want now?*

Basu entered the specs into his iKatana and then held the cyber-frog out of the window. It pushed off of Basu's palm and flew in a downward direction. The bus followed.

There was a loud bang on the roof of the hover-bus. Then another bang. Basu looked up, wondering what was happening. Then he saw them. Gomen ninjas were raining out of the sky. They jumped from the surrounding windows and landed on top of the bus. First there were just a few, then a dozen.

"We're under attack," Chiya shouted through the door, pounding on it with her tiny white fist.

Basu grunted at the door.

He tapped a message for Oekai into his iKatana and clicked *send*. The message had his coordinates and situation. He knew his company would send backup as soon as they could.

A Gomen ninja burst through the side window and flipped into an attack stance. Before Basu could strike, the Gomen tossed three pulse-shuriken into the dashboard. The shuriken sent a wave of electricity that short-circuited all of the electrical components in the dash, including the controls.

The hover-bus started going down.

Basu sliced the ninja across the chest and then drop-kicked him through the wall of the bus. As the ninja fell into the abyss, he launched a grappling hook at Basu. It caught onto a chunk of fat in his chest.

The ninja reeled himself in at the speed of a dart, flying back inside through the hole. He pulled three more shuriken out of his belt, holding them in the spaces between his four fingers. Then Basu cut off his head, before the shuriken had a chance to do any more damage.

He wobbled back to the controls, but they were burnt. He couldn't work the steering wheel. He couldn't work the brake. Peeking his head out the window, he saw more and more ninjas falling out of the sky onto the bus.

In the storefront area, Basu found Chiya taking on five Gomens all by herself. There were two others on the floor, already dead.

Chiya's lightweight body cartwheeled backward three times, slicing the throat of one of the ninjas on the way.

She pulled a small knife out of her boot and tossed it into a Gomen's chest, right through the pocket of his polo shirt.

At first, Basu thought she was doing really well. She had killed two of them in under a minute. But then he saw the gashes on her belly and the stab wounds between her ribs under her arm. She had been hit several times. Two of them were fatal wounds.

She was struck again across her tiny anime nose and she tottered back, breathing rapidly. The angle of the bus was becoming sharper, and she was having difficulty keeping herself upright. She looked over at Basu.

"What are you waiting for?" she cried. "Help me."

Basu grunted at her. Then he twisted his hip to show her the wound she had given him. He folded his arms and watched her.

"Asshole!" she said, as a ninja flew at her.

She blocked his attack, then stabbed him in the eye. The Gomen screamed as she pulled his eye out like a meatball on a fork. She yanked the eyeball off of her switchblade with her teeth and spit it at Basu.

The obese ninja looked down at the eyeball and then up at Chiya as she gutted the screaming one-eyed man from his ribs to his scrotum. Then Basu stepped away from them and looked out of a window. The bus was coming down fast. Basu had to balance at a seventy-degree angle to keep from falling backward.

Chiya stabbed one of the ninjas in the face, through his cheek into the brain. Then she slipped on her own blood and wobbled. The last Gomen ninja took the opportunity to fly at her with his sword, pointing straight for her heart. Chiya shrieked.

The blade only entered her skin one centimeter. Basu

caught the Gomen's iKatana with his bare hand, stopping it from going all the way in. His palm dripped blood down the Gomen's blade. The Gomen found himself shaking as he looked into Basu's cold ink eyes.

Basu grunted at the man, then he disemboweled him with his own sword.

"Why are we going down?" Chiya yelled, holding onto a kitchen cabinet.

"Pulse shuriken," Basu said.

Chiya kicked her refrigerator.

"We need to put it into manual," she said. "I can do it if we have enough time."

"We don't," Basu said.

"I have to try," she said.

Basu nodded.

They balanced their way through the plummeting bus back to the cockpit and Chiya went straight to work. She held her wounds as she took a toolkit out of the glove box and crawled under the dashboard to assess the situation.

As she worked, Basu looked out of the window. The light outside was getting darker and darker as they went down. If the surrounding buildings were just a little closer and they weren't falling so quickly he would have been able to jump to safety. But it would be impossible to even try. Everything counted on Chiya getting the controls fixed. He could see the ground beginning to come into view. It was getting bigger and bigger. They were going down fast.

"Hurry," Basu said.

Chiya's fingers were slippery with blood as she pulled out electrical components and rearranged wires. It didn't seem to Basu that she was making any progress at all.

"It'll be just a second," she said.

Basu could see the details of the ground now. He could see the miles of garbage that had piled up. There were mountains of green garbage bags, crushed vehicles, building debris, and even dead bodies that had been tossed out of windows by uncaring family members.

Basu grunted down at Chiya.

"Got it," she said.

Chiya jumped up to the controls and pulled back on the wheel. Basu balanced himself as the hover-bus straightened out.

"We're not going to make it," Chiya said as she saw the mountains of garbage coming at her.

"Shut up," Basu said.

The hover-bus rammed through a peak of trash and they both jerked backward. The wheel slipped out of Chiya's bloody fingers and she fell on her knees. Basu grabbed the wheel and tried to straighten the vehicle. It hit another mountain of garbage and then flipped onto its side.

Chiya screamed as she was tossed against a wall, breaking her wrist and pulverizing three ribs.

Basu was able to keep his balance as the hover-bus hit a level plateau of garbage. The trash was so compressed that it was as solid as concrete. The front of the bus hit first, crushing the hood on impact and launching it into a roll. Sparks flew into the air as the bus spiraled across the plateau. It fell off of the edge and tumbled down a jagged slope into a basin.

ROKU

Basu pulled debris out of his folds of fat. The windshield had broken open and filled the cockpit with decades-old trash. His nostrils quivered with the scent of salty mold and tangy copper. He stood up and examined his iKatana, making sure that it was still working adequately.

He saw Chiya laying in a mess of broken dinner plates and petrified diapers. She was crinkled like newspaper, bones broken in so many places that they looked saw-like. Her arms were twisted into a knot. Her chest was caved in.

In order to make animese people more lightweight, cosmetic surgeons reduced the density of their bones. This made them lighter and more flexible, but it also made them a lot more fragile.

Chiya only had a few minutes left. Basu put her ragdoll hand into his and kissed her on her forehead with his thick crusty lips.

"I always thought I could change you," she said, her voice rough and whispery. It sounded like she had butterfly wings in her vocal chords. "I always thought I could cure you, get you back into shape. I always thought I could be with my Keigo again."

Basu grunted at her.

"If only I had my Keigo back . . ." she said. "*He* would have been willing to make a change and leave this city with me."

Basu grunted softly.

55

"But there's no changing Basu," she said. "There's no changing this fat piece of shit."

He held her crumpled hand and waited for her to die. As he stared into her big wet eyes, he wondered what she saw when she looked at him. They'd known each other for a long time, but they never really spoke to each other much. The rare occasions that they spent the night together, they mostly just sat in silence. It was as if Chiya had filled in her own conversations during those silent moments. It was as if Chiya had been in a serious relationship with him for years, but she was the only one who knew about it.

As consciousness dripped out of her anime eyes, all Basu could do to comfort her was grunt.

Outside the wrecked hover-bus, the air was thick. Basu looked above him. The buildings stretched so far up that he couldn't see any sky beyond them. The lighting was very dim, but Basu was still able to see everything clearly. There were many lights in the buildings three hundred feet up, but the buildings close to the ground were dark and empty. Deserted. It had been decades since anyone had lived this close to the ground.

A wave of pressure rose inside of Basu's guts, causing him to freeze in his tracks. He had to take a crap. Another major setback of eating so much food was that he had to shit constantly, and it almost always came on suddenly, when least expected.

"Not now," Basu told himself.

But he knew he couldn't hold it. It wasn't the first time he had a bathroom emergency in the wrong place, at the wrong time. He thought about using the bathroom on the crashed hover-bus, but decided against it. The Gomen ninja would surely be surrounding the area at any moment. Nothing was more difficult than trying to defend attackers while glued to a toilet seat.

Basu hobbled between the garbage hills until he found a hidden cavern within a mountain of trash. He watched for Gomen ninjas as he pulled down his pants, making sure they hadn't arrived on the scene yet, not that he would have been able to stop even if they were.

His bowels exploded across the ancient soda cans and broken electronics. When he looked back, he saw that half of what was coming out of him was blood. A thick bright red blood that splashed in such a way that it appeared to have been punched out of him. Although the blood was possibly from the stab wounds to his belly, bloody stool was not uncommon for Basu.

Because his diet consisted of large quantities of unhealthy fattening foods with hardly any fiber, his colon and intestines were in horrible shape. They were full of hemorrhoids and polyps, which were often torn open by all the stool passing through him, causing rectal bleeding.

As he finished shitting and wiped himself with an old dirt-caked hairpiece, he stood up and took a few steps, then had to go to the bathroom again. This time it wasn't just shit and blood that came out of him; there was also a fishy yellow discharge oozing down the back of his thighs. The rancid slime was from an infection of the hemorrhoids, which he got from time to time. Open wounds in the intestines very easily became infected.

Basu wiped the thick fluid off of his legs with a half-melted Frisbee, and recoiled at the rotten smell when he brought it up to his nose. Whenever the fishy goop came out of him, Basu was forced to recognize what his horrible diet was doing to his body. Eventually, it was going to kill him.

As Basu came out of the cavern and examined his surroundings, he saw a pink cyber-chickadee fly past him with a big cartoon smile on its face. He grunted with confusion. Then he looked up and saw Crow in the sky, flying overhead on a hover-bike, chasing after the chickadee. Basu then realized the chickadee was an iPet that was going after Oki.

Basu leapt thirty feet into the air across a garbage ravine and went after the floppy pink chickadee. He landed knee-deep in refuse. Then he launched himself upward again, trying to ignore the pain within his intestines.

Crow sliced through the sky above him, his black tie rippling over his shoulder. He pointed his beak downward at Basu and squawked at him.

The obese ninja jumped into the air and swung his iKatana. Crow's hover-bike tilted sideways to avoid it. As Basu fell back down, Crow tossed three mine-shuriken at him. The projectiles exploded at Basu's feet. Rubbish burst into the air and a mountain of garbage avalanched on top of him.

By the time Basu pulled himself out of the refuse, the

pink chickadee was too far away for him to see, and Crow was out of his range of attack. Four more Gomen ninja flew overhead on hover-bikes, catching up with their leader.

Basu got right back to his feet and jumped frantically through the garbage landscape after them. His breath was becoming heavy, his heart was feeling squeezed within his chest, and his intestines felt so rotten that he imagined they were ready to turn into mush and slide out of his rectum.

By the time he caught up to Crow and the Gomen ninja, Basu was ready to collapse. He was a powerful killing machine when fighting in quick bursts, but he didn't have a lot of stamina. Running long distances took a lot out of him.

When Crow saw the state of Basu, he squawked a laugh. "You're not the warrior you used to be, Keigo."

When Basu looked up, he saw Oki was with Crow. The boy was backed against a wall of ancient washing machines. The wrecked hover-scooter he had used to make his escape was on the ground twenty feet away. He was holding Basu's smiling cyber-frog in his arms like a teddybear, tears falling down his cheeks. When Oki saw the obese ninja, his face lit up.

"Bus!" Oki cried.

Crow held the struggling child still.

Basu stood up and held out his iKatana in one hand, his other hand holding the stab wound on his hip. Even after he developed his weight problem, he had never failed a mission before. He would not let Crow get away with the piggy bank.

"Kill him off before he catches his breath," Crow told the four Gomen ninjas next to him.

The Gomen came at him quickly. The way they weaved through each other, flying like jets in formation, Basu could tell these were not ordinary ninjas. They were elite assassins. One of them wore a blue hood tucked into his polo shirt, one wore a red hood, another wore yellow, and the last wore purple.

Although he would have no trouble dispatching any elite assassin in single combat, Basu knew it would be suicide to fight a group of them while they were in formation. In any other circumstance he would have chosen to retreat and wait for backup to arrive, but this time he didn't have any other option but to fight them head on. If he could kill just one of them, that would weaken their formation enough to give Basu a chance. This was the strategy he chose as they swooped in on him like vultures.

The lead assassin with the red hood broke away from the group and darted toward Basu as the others circled around him. Once he was in range, Basu took his hand from his hip wound and splashed blood into Red Hood's eyes. Then he swung his iKatana.

As the iKatana was about to make contact with Red Hood, Basu's heart began to pump hard in his chest, as if the organ was struggling to break free from his ribcage. The force of Basu's attack weakened. It felt to Basu as if his arm had started moving in slow motion. His horrible blood pressure had finally caught up to him.

As the blade came down toward Red Hood, the assassin's body exploded into black smoke and disappeared. Basu's sword fell through the smoke without making contact. Then Red Hood reappeared on the right side of Basu and drove his iKatana through the obese man's sword arm. Basu cried out, pulling his arm off of the blade. Then he sloppily swung his sword at the assassin, breathing rapidly as his heart pounded. Red Hood disappeared again.

Before Basu could see him reappearing on his left, the assassin knocked Basu's iKatana out of his hand and then pierced the blade into his enormous belly.

"Bus!" cried Oki, struggling in Crow's arms as the morbidly obese ninja fell to the ground.

SHICHI

The assassins hovered over Basu as a pool of blood formed beneath his mountain of flesh. Once they agreed he was dead, they started back toward Crow. But Basu was not yet dead. He had so much fat on his body that even though the assassin's sword went all the way into his body, the blade still wasn't long enough to hit any major organs. The morbidly obese ninja pushed himself up onto his hands and knees.

When Crow saw him struggling to stand, he found it amusing. "You still have fight in you, eh Keigo? How many times must I have you killed before you actually die, you fat piece of shit?"

Basu grunted. It was a soft wheezing grunt. As his heart continued to pound, rivers of sweat poured down his mounds of flesh, mixing with his blood, drenching his clothing.

Crow flicked his beak at his men and the elite assassins returned to finish the ninja.

As the assassins closed in around him, Basu got to his feet, staggering like a fat drunk. Without a sword, he would have to fight them barehanded. The blue-hooded assassin whipped around him, crossing the yellow-hooded assassin who whipped around to the other side. They were spinning their swords like batons.

It was Purple Hood who struck first. He went for a

decapitation strike, aiming for his neck, but Basu bent his body all the way back in order to dodge it. As his head leaned back, Basu's belly swung forward, slamming into the assassin's chest, knocking him ten feet off the ground. When Purple Hood fell, he landed on his feet unfazed and charged back into action.

Blue Hood spit glowing green sludge on the back of Basu's head. Like acid, the radioactive spit melted through his hair, burning his flesh. Green smoke billowed out of the wound. Basu charged head-first into Yellow Hood, hoping to knock the assassin down and wipe the toxic sludge off on him at the same time. But just as he made impact, the yellow-hooded assassin's skin turned a white color and became as hard as stone.

When Basu's head slammed into Yellow Hood's rock flesh, blood sprayed from his forehead and he tottered backward, his vision spinning, his rolls of fat flopping and jiggling as he staggered. He wasn't sure if his dizziness was due to concussion or because his heart was becoming tighter and tighter inside of his chest.

Blue Hood slashed Basu across the back as he was falling. Then smoke exploded in front of him as Red Hood appeared, slashing Basu across the chest. The four assassins surrounded him, taking turns striking, slashing into his hundreds of pounds of blubber. They didn't go for his head or heart, just for his rolls of fat, as if they were toying with him, making a game of it.

Oki watched from the crow man's clutches as gash after gash appeared on Basu's body. The boy looked up at Crow, who was watching with wide-eyed pleasure, licking the edges of his black beak with his pink human tongue, savoring the demise of his old friend.

As he was being sliced to shreds, Basu felt the fishy yellow discharge oozing out of his rectum into his pants. That was the final straw. He finally felt utterly hopelessly pathetic. He thought about how much of a wreck he had become, how much of a grotesque pile of shit he was.

While staggering between the assassins, Basu grunted at himself. He wondered if he was just kidding himself when he thought he could still be a great ninja after gaining over five hundred excess pounds. Being that freakishly obese was a serious handicap for a human being. Of course he couldn't take on the likes of the Gomen Corporation. He didn't have the stamina or the agility of a ninja anymore. He was nothing but a blob with a sword.

But as Red Hood stuck him in the ass with his sword, Basu snapped out of it. He stopped feeling sorry for himself. He wasn't an overweight pile of shit. He was Basu. He was seven hundred pounds of total destruction. Nobody could defeat Basu. Not Crow, not anyone.

Once Basu became morbidly obese, he decided to turn his weakness into a strength. He understood putting seven hundred pounds behind an attack was an incredibly powerful blow. He understood that he could kill a man just by landing on top of him. There were things he could do that no other ninja could do. He refused to give up and die. He would not let the assassins defeat him, nor Crow, nor his lack of stamina or his pounding heart. He would not give up. He was ninja. He was Basu.

At that moment, the four assassins dove forward to

deal their final blows, but the morbidly obese ninja leapt high into the air. As their swords clacked together, the assassins looked up at the man-blimp in the air above them. Three of the assassins dodged out of the way as Basu came tumbling back toward the earth.

The fourth assassin, Yellow Hood, didn't notice Basu's enormous body falling on him until the last second. Yellow Hood used his power to change his skin into rock, to protect him on impact. But as Basu landed on Yellow Hood, the rock skin was not enough. Basu's massive weight crushed Yellow Hood's rock body into the ground, his innards splattering out of cracks in his sides.

When Basu stood, brushing guts and crumbles of rock skin from his belly, he stared down Crow. He wiped the green toxic sludge from the back of his head, pulling off a wad of his melted scalp and tossed it aside. The acid had burned all the way to the bone, exposing part of his skull. He paid it no mind.

"Kill him," Crow yelled.

Red Hood hesitated. Without all four team members, the assassins felt lost, flawed.

"I said kill him!

Red Hood and Purple Hood charged the ninja. Blue Hood circled around his back. Red Hood disappeared into black smoke and then reappeared with his sword mere inches from Basu's throat. But the sword stopped just before piercing the flesh. Red Hood was staring into Basu's eyes. The morbidly obese ninja grunted at him. Seeing Basu's hands resting on his waist, Red Hood wondered what had stopped his attack. He looked down to see that it was Basu's flabby breasts that had caught the blade, reaching up like an extra set of limbs.

Then, as if he had more sets of limbs, several rolls of fat launched like fists at Red Hood, punching him in the chest and stomach. The fat rolls pummeled him repeatedly until Basu's breasts released the blade, wrapped around his throat, and snapped the assassin's neck.

As Blue Hood came up behind, Basu grabbed him by the mouth just as he was about to spit another glob of the green toxic sludge. With the acid trapped inside of Blue Hood's mouth, it began eating through his cheeks and tongue. Basu glared at him, squeezed his face harder as the man struggled to break free. When the toxic fluid drained down the back of his mouth, Blue Hood's throat melted open, releasing a river of blood down his chest. Basu left him writhing on the ground.

The last assassin, Purple Hood, trembled beneath the mighty Basu. He used his secret assassin power. Purple Hood's body multiplied into twelve different clones of himself that spread out and surrounded Basu. Only one of them was the real Purple Hood. The others were just illusions.

But his illusions could not hide him from Basu. The obese ninja had grown an acute sense of smell ever since his brain became guided by his stomach. He could smell which one was the real purple-hooded assassin. Basu went straight up to him and picked him up in a bear hug.

As Basu crushed the assassin's ribcage, he smelled something appealing in the man's sweat. Purple Hood, for some reason, smelled a bit like cheeseburgers to Basu. Realizing he was behind on his calorie intake for the day, Basu decided to indulge himself. He ripped open Purple Hood's polo shirt and bit into the flesh on his arm.

Purple Hood screamed as Basu began to eat him alive.

Large round teeth ripped at the flesh on the assassin's body, trying to find some delicious high calorie fats among the disgustingly lean meat. Basu had never resorted to cannibalism in the past, but now realized that it was a potential source of calories in an emergency situation.

When the last elite assassin fell dead in the ninja's arms, Basu retrieved his iKatana and stumbled toward Crow. Bloody sweat poured down his massive frame. A chunk of human fat dangled from his lips.

Although he knew Basu had won the battle, Crow had already lost interest in the fight and had turned his attention to Oki. He had the unlocking mechanism in his hand and was about to put it to the boy's chest

Crow looked over his shoulder and blinked his beady eyes at his old friend.

"Stop," Basu told him, while chewing on the chunk of fat.

Crow stood up.

"Or what?" Crow said.

Basu swallowed the meat, then ran forward a few steps and raised his sword.

Crow let out a birdlike chuckle.

"You can't kill me," Crow said. "I'm an executive."

Then Crow went back to the device.

Basu lunged at Crow and sliced his arm off. The severed arm fell to the ground, still holding the unlocking mechanism. Crow shrieked. Bird blood sprayed down his suit and feathers.

"What the hell are you doing?" Crow squawked. "You'll be executed for this!"

Basu twirled his iKatana at Crow.

"Not if I don't kill you," Basu said.

Crow let out a shrill squawk and whipped out his chain sickle. He swung it over his head and then launched it at Basu.

The obese ninja just stood there as the chain sickle wrapped around his body and then hooked into his hip. Crow shrieked a laugh and then tugged on his chain.

Nothing happened. Crow's laughter came to a halt. He put all of his strength into jerking on the chain, but Basu wouldn't budge. Crow looked at Basu with confused beady eyes.

Crow had always had the strength to toss around men twice his size after hooking them with his chain, but what Crow hadn't calculated was that Basu wasn't twice his size. He was over five times his size.

Basu glanced down at the chain and then grunted at him.

Crow quickly tried to pull the spool of chain out of the sleeve of his suit, but Basu was already wrapping his fingers around it.

There was a loud squawking cry as Basu tugged the chain as hard as he could, reeling the one-armed bird man toward him. Crow landed on the end of Basu's iKatana. It went through his belly in the same spot that Crow had stabbed Keigo three years ago. He coughed blood out of his black beak as he slid off of the blade.

It was a painful, incapacitating wound, but the bird man would survive it.

HACHI

As Basu untangled the chain from his flesh, Crow crawled with one arm back to the unlocking mechanism. Basu thought it was just like his old friend to never give up.

Before Crow could get to his severed arm, Basu pried the device out of the fingers and curled it into his armpit.

"Pathetic," Basu said to Crow.

Then he took Oki by the hand and walked him away from the wounded animal.

"Pathetic?" Crow shrieked. "Look at you."

Basu kept walking.

"All you can do is eat and destroy." Crow's beak leaned into a puddle of his blood as he yelled. "You're the worst kind of human being there is. You act like you care. You pretend that you have honor. But the only thing you are good at is consuming and destroying everything around you."

The morbidly obese ninja grunted as he walked away.

Then Basu was surrounded by two dozen ninjas. They stood silently like grim reapers, wearing all black clothing. They were from the Oekai Corporation. Oki looked up at

Basu and the obese ninja took his hand, held it tight.

They stepped toward the lead ninja of the unit. The ninja stepped forward and unfolded a document. He held it up so that Basu could read it. The document was clearance to execute the Gomen executive, Crow. Basu looked down at the ninja and nodded his head, then he shoved him out of his way.

The Oekai ninjas turned their attentions toward Crow, who squawked a whimper and tried to crawl to his feet with his single arm. They drew swords from their scabbards and closed in on him.

Basu took Oki away from the scene. He held him close to his greasy flesh, and led him down a hill of garbage. They got far enough away that they didn't hear Crow's final screams.

At the bottom of the hill, there was a patch of dirt twenty feet long. Basu let go of the boy's hand so he could wander. He knew how much the boy wanted to see what the ground looked like.

Oki stepped cautiously across the soil, the smiling holo-frog hopping casually behind him. Then he looked back at Basu.

"This is it?" Oki said. "This is the ground?"

Basu grunted.

"It's so boring," Oki said.

Basu approached the boy and knelt down to him.

"I told you there was nothing special about it," Basu said.

Oki scanned the dirt, shaking his head. He was so unimpressed that he didn't know what else to say about it. He looked up at the Oekai company ships hovering in the air above them and looked back at the ninjas coming down the hill from behind.

"They are here to open you up," said Basu.

Oki nodded.

"Are you going to allow them to do their duty?" Basu asked. "Will you die with dignity?"

Oki nodded.

Basu wiped a tear from the boy's eye and grunted at him. Then he said, "I'm proud of you."

Oki nodded and took the unlocking mechanism from Basu. Then he grunted up at him.

Basu took the boy by the hand and led him up the garbage hill to a group of executives heading toward them. The head executive, an old man with a tall wrinkled forehead, waved at his men to take the boy. Then he went to Basu.

"Excellent work, Basu," his boss said.

Basu grunted, paying more attention to Oki than his employer. The boy's eyes were locked on Basu as the ninjas took him away.

"With this information we will finally get ahead of the Gomen Corporation," said the boss. "We owe it all to you."

A technician knelt down to Oki and put the unlocking mechanism to his chest. Oki tried to act as courageous as possible while the device was attached to his iron torso.

"What is the information, anyway?" Basu asked.

The executive frowned at Basu. "It's not like you to ask such questions."

"Just curious."

"Well, since you did such a good job I'll tell you this one time." The executive looked over at Oki and smiled. "Inside of that piggy bank are designs for a program that will be the hot new iPalm app of the year."

"What kind of app?"

The executive's voice became giddy. "It allows the iPalm customer to instantly change the color of their fingernails. There are over 2,000 colors and patterns to choose from."

"That's it?"

"What do you mean *that's it*? Do you know how popular that's going to be with teenage girls? We are going to make a fortune!"

Basu's face was turning red. That was what he had been risking his life for? That was what the two companies were at war over? That was why so many ninjas had to die? That was the information Oki must die for? It was too absurd for Basu to accept.

As the technician hovering over Oki fidgeted with the unlocking mechanism, the boy looked up at Basu with tears in his eyes. Basu could tell he didn't want to die for the sake of duty and honor. Oki was only doing it for Basu, because it was what Basu wanted him to do. But Basu realized that he was wrong. It was not honorable to accept your fate. If Basu accepted his fate he never would have continued as a ninja after being infected with the nano-poison. He would have given up and died.

Just before the technician found the right combination, Basu flew through the crowd of Oekai employees and sliced the unlocking mechanism in half. The technician fell backward in shock. Then he shoved the ninjas away from the boy, threatening them with his iKatana.

Oki looked up at Basu with a big smile. Basu looked down at him and grunted.

"What do you think you're doing, Basu?" said his boss.

All of the Oekai ninjas followed after their boss. The technicians and other executives kept a safe distance.

"I won't let you kill him," Basu said.

"I never expected this from you," said his boss. "In one day, you've actually become attached to this boy? You of all people would betray your company, of which you've sworn an oath to obey, for the sake of some worthless piggy bank?"

Basu grunted.

"Don't be fooled by his appearance," said his boss. "I know you think you're doing the right thing, but he's just a piggy bank. He doesn't matter. He's not even a real child."

"What do you mean?"

"Piggy banks aren't born," said the boss. "They are grown in a lab. How old do you think this boy is? Seven years old? Eight years old?" He shook his head. "No, he's been alive for less than four months. He can never grow older and probably won't live for more than a year. He's not worth throwing away your life."

Basu looked down at Oki. The boy stared up at him with watering eyes.

"Hand him over and I'll pretend this never happened," said his boss. "Otherwise, you'll be fired. Right here, right now."

When Basu looked at Oki, he couldn't see a lab-grown four-month-old machine. All he saw was a boy who was frightened, who wanted to live.

"Well, what will it be?"

Basu grunted.

"Is that a *yes* grunt or a *no* grunt?"

Basu leaned in close. "It's a *fuck you* grunt."

His boss rolled his eyes. "A pity, Basu. A real pity." Then he stepped back and said, "Okay, then. You're fired."

The ninjas surrounding them drew their swords and pointed them at Basu. The ninjas didn't need their boss to spell out the fact that he had just ordered them to kill the obese ninja.

"Back off," Basu told the ninjas.

They cowered around him, but didn't lower their swords. All of them knew how strong Basu was. Every single one of them dreaded the idea of taking on the deadliest ninja their company had ever known. They knew that if they fought Basu he would kill the majority (or all) of them for sure, but if they disobeyed orders they would be executed. It was a no-win situation for them.

"What are you all waiting for?" the executive yelled. "Kill him."

They did nothing.

Basu smiled.

Then he cut the executive's head from his shoulders in one quick swipe.

The ninjas still did nothing. They just watched as their boss's body plopped on the ground next to them.

Basu glared at the ninjas. They stepped back.

"I've just killed your boss," he told the ninjas. "He won't be able to fire any of you now. All you have to do is walk away."

The ninjas hesitated. With their boss dead, they could quit their positions without risk of being executed by the board of directors. Quitting would be dishonorable and no company would ever hire them again, but they would still have their lives.

"So what's it going to be?" Basu said.

One of the ninjas dropped his sword. The others looked at him. He pulled the hood off of his face, dropped it, and walked away. A second ninja dropped his sword and left. Then a third.

"What are you doing?" said the other executives. "Are you all mad?"

A fourth and a fifth dropped their swords and left.

"Where's your honor? Where's your ninja code?"

Then the rest of them dropped their swords. They all walked off, back toward the ship. The technicians followed after.

"Cowards! Fucking cowards!" the executives cried. "He's just one man!"

Then the executives realized it was just them and Basu. They stopped yelling at the ninjas and began to inch backward. Basu took one step in their direction and they fled, running back to the ship to get a ride back with the recently retired ninjas.

KYUU

It was just Oki and Basu left on the trash mountain, standing like grubby statues in the ocean of waste.

The morbidly obese ninja stared up at the sky, the buildings so tall he could hardly see even a speck of blue. Oki looked up at him.

"Are you okay?" Oki said, pointing at all the wounds on Basu's body.

Basu grunted and glanced down at the wounds for a second, then shrugged. Even though many of them were deep gashes with chunks of meat hanging from bloody gaping holes, Basu thought of them as nothing more than mere scratches.

"So what do we do now?" Oki asked.

Basu grunted, still looking up at the sky.

"How are we going to get back up there?"

Basu grunted, then squeezed a package of mayonnaise into his mouth.

"Do you really want to go back up there?" Basu asked with a mouthful of white goop.

Oki looked down at his metal chest.

"No, I suppose not," he said. "But where should we go instead?"

Basu let out a long grunt. Then a short one.

"Let's just walk," Basu said, "and see where it takes us."

Oki grunted at him. A high-pitched little boy grunt.

The tiny metal boy and the enormous blob of a ninja walked hand in hand through the dimly lit valley of garbage. They didn't know if the long-abandoned road would lead them out of the city or just go on forever, but they kept walking. Hopefully, eventually, it would lead them somewhere new, somewhere better, somewhere with all the high-calorie foods Basu could eat and all the fun Oki could have.

Neither of them were going to live for much longer, but with the little time they had left, one thing was for sure: they were going to spend it together.

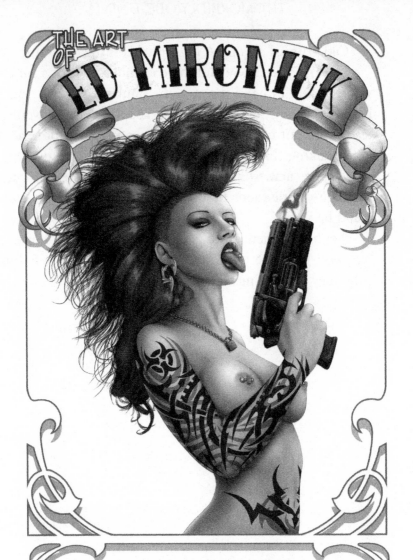

THE ART OF ED MIRONIUK

48 full color pages of kinky and kutie pin-up girls with a rough and ready attitude hand signed with original one of a kind sketch
$40
http://edmironiuk.bigcartel.com/

"Fetish pinup girls that are as interesting and strange as they are sexy. The more you see of Ed Mironiuk's art, the more it will attach itself to you. This book is a must-buy."
Carlton Mellick III

ABOUT THE AUTHOR

Carlton Mellick III is one of the leading authors
in the new *Bizarro* genre uprising. Since 2001,
his surreal counterculture novels have drawn
an international cult following despite the fact
that they have been shunned by most libraries
and corporate bookstores. He lives in Portland,
OR, the bizarro fiction mecca.

Visit him online at **www.carltonmellick.com**

Bizarro books

CATALOG   SPRING 2011

Bizarro Books publishes under the following imprints:

www.rawdogscreamingpress.com

www.eraserheadpress.com

www.afterbirthbooks.com

www.swallowdownpress.com

For all your Bizarro needs visit:

WWW.BIZARROCENTRAL.COM

Introduce yourselves to the bizarro fiction genre and all of its authors with the Bizarro Starter Kit series. Each volume features short novels and short stories by ten of the leading bizarro authors, designed to give you a perfect sampling of the genre for only $10.

BB-0X1
"The Bizarro Starter Kit"
(Orange)
Featuring D. Harlan Wilson, Carlton Mellick III, Jeremy Robert Johnson, Kevin L Donihe, Gina Ranalli, Andre Duza, Vincent W. Sakowski, Steve Beard, John Edward Lawson, and Bruce Taylor.
236 pages $10

BB-0X2
"The Bizarro Starter Kit"
(Blue)
Featuring Ray Fracalossy, Jeremy C. Shipp, Jordan Krall, Mykle Hansen, Andersen Prunty, Eckhard Gerdes, Bradley Sands, Steve Aylett, Christian TeBordo, and Tony Rauch. **244 pages $10**

BB-0X2
"The Bizarro Starter Kit"
(Purple)
Featuring Russell Edson, Athena Villaverde, David Agranoff, Matthew Revert, Andrew Goldfarb, Jeff Burk, Garrett Cook, Kris Saknussemm, Cody Goodfellow, and Cameron Pierce **264 pages $10**

BB-001"The Kafka Effekt" D. Harlan Wilson - A collection of forty-four irreal short stories loosely written in the vein of Franz Kafka, with more than a pinch of William S. Burroughs sprinkled on top. **211 pages $14**

BB-002 "Satan Burger" Carlton Mellick III - The cult novel that put Carlton Mellick III on the map ... Six punks get jobs at a fast food restaurant owned by the devil in a city violently overpopulated by surreal alien cultures. **236 pages $14**

BB-003 "Some Things Are Better Left Unplugged" Vincent Sakwoski - Join The Man and his Nemesis, the obese tabby, for a nightmare roller coaster ride into this postmodern fantasy. **152 pages $10**

BB-004 "Shall We Gather At the Garden?" Kevin L Donihe - Donihe's Debut novel. Midgets take over the world, The Church of Lionel Richie vs. The Church of the Byrds, plant porn and more! **244 pages $14**

BB-005 "Razor Wire Pubic Hair" Carlton Mellick III - A genderless humandildo is purchased by a razor dominatrix and brought into her nightmarish world of bizarre sex and mutilation. **176 pages $11**

BB-006 "Stranger on the Loose" D. Harlan Wilson - The fiction of Wilson's 2nd collection is planted in the soil of normalcy, but what grows out of that soil is a dark, witty, otherworldly jungle... **228 pages $14**

BB-007 "The Baby Jesus Butt Plug" Carlton Mellick III - Using clones of the Baby Jesus for anal sex will be the hip sex fetish of the future. **92 pages $10**

BB-008 "Fishyfleshed" Carlton Mellick III - The world of the past is an illogical flatland lacking in dimension and color, a sick-scape of crispy squid people wandering the desert for no apparent reason. **260 pages $14**

BB-009 **"Dead Bitch Army" Andre Duza** - Step into a world filled with racist teenagers, cannibals, 100 warped Uncle Sams, automobiles with razor-sharp teeth, living graffiti, and a pissed-off zombie bitch out for revenge. **344 pages $16**

BB-010 **"The Menstruating Mall" Carlton Mellick III** - "The Breakfast Club meets Chopping Mall as directed by David Lynch." - Brian Keene **212 pages $12**

BB-011 **"Angel Dust Apocalypse" Jeremy Robert Johnson** - Meth-heads, man-made monsters, and murderous Neo-Nazis. "Seriously amazing short stories..." - Chuck Palahniuk, author of Fight Club **184 pages $11**

BB-012 **"Ocean of Lard" Kevin L Donihe / Carlton Mellick III** - A parody of those old Choose Your Own Adventure kid's books about some very odd pirates sailing on a sea made of animal fat. **176 pages $12**

BB-015 **"Foop!" Chris Genoa** - Strange happenings are going on at Dactyl, Inc, the world's first and only time travel tourism company.
"A surreal pie in the face!" - Christopher Moore **300 pages $14**

BB-020 **"Punk Land" Carlton Mellick III** - In the punk version of Heaven, the anarchist utopia is threatened by corporate fascism and only Goblin, Mortician's sperm, and a blue-mohawked female assassin named Shark Girl can stop them. **284 pages $15**

BB-021 **"Pseudo-City" D. Harlan Wilson** - Pseudo-City exposes what waits in the bathroom stall, under the manhole cover and in the corporate boardroom, all in a way that can only be described as mind-bogglingly irreal. **220 pages $16**

BB-023 **"Sex and Death In Television Town" Carlton Mellick III** - In the old west, a gang of hermaphrodite gunslingers take refuge from a demon plague in Telos: a town where its citizens have televisions instead of heads. **184 pages $12**

BB-027 **"Siren Promised" Jeremy Robert Johnson & Alan M Clark**
- Nominated for the Bram Stoker Award. A potent mix of bad drugs, bad dreams, brutal bad guys, and surreal/incredible art by Alan M. Clark. **190 pages $13**

BB-030 **"Grape City" Kevin L. Donihe** - More Donihe-style comedic bizarro about a demon named Charles who is forced to work a minimum wage job on Earth after Hell goes out of business. **108 pages $10**

BB-031**"Sea of the Patchwork Cats" Carlton Mellick III** - A quiet dreamlike tale set in the ashes of the human race. For Mellick enthusiasts who also adore The Twilight Zone. **112 pages $10**

BB-032 **"Extinction Journals" Jeremy Robert Johnson** - An uncanny voyage across a newly nuclear America where one man must confront the problems associated with loneliness, insane dieties, radiation, love, and an ever-evolving cockroach suit with a mind of its own. **104 pages $10**

BB-034 **"The Greatest Fucking Moment in Sports" Kevin L. Donihe**
- In the tradition of the surreal anti-sitcom Get A Life comes a tale of triumph and agape love from the master of comedic bizarro. **108 pages $10**

BB-035 **"The Troublesome Amputee" John Edward Lawson** - Disturbing verse from a man who truly believes nothing is sacred and intends to prove it. **104 pages $9**

BB-037 **"The Haunted Vagina" Carlton Mellick III** - It's difficult to love a woman whose vagina is a gateway to the world of the dead. **132 pages $10**

BB-042 **"Teeth and Tongue Landscape" Carlton Mellick III** - On a planet made out of meat, a socially-obsessive monophobic man tries to find his place amongst the strange creatures and communities that he comes across. **110 pages $10**

BB-043 **"War Slut" Carlton Mellick III** - Part "1984," part "Waiting for Godot," and part action horror video game adaptation of John Carpenter's "The Thing." **116 pages $10**

BB-045 **"Dr. Identity" D. Harlan Wilson** - Follow the Dystopian Duo on a killing spree of epic proportions through the irreal postcapitalist city of Bliptown where time ticks sideways, artificial Bug-Eyed Monsters punish citizens for consumer-capitalist lethargy, and ultraviolence is as essential as a daily multivitamin. **208 pages $15**

BB-047 **"Sausagey Santa" Carlton Mellick III** - A bizarro Christmas tale featuring Santa as a piratey mutant with a body made of sausages. 124 pages $10

BB-048 **"Misadventures in a Thumbnail Universe" Vincent Sakowski** - Dive deep into the surreal and satirical realms of neo-classical Blender Fiction, filled with television shoes and flesh-filled skies. **120 pages $10**

BB-049 **"Vacation" Jeremy C. Shipp** - Blueblood Bernard Johnson left his boring life behind to go on The Vacation, a year-long corporate sponsored odyssey. But instead of seeing the world, Bernard is captured by terrorists, becomes a key figure in secret drug wars, and, worse, doesn't once miss his secure American Dream. **160 pages $14**

BB-053 **"Ballad of a Slow Poisoner" Andrew Goldfarb** Millford Mutter-wurst sat down on a Tuesday to take his afternoon tea, and made the unpleasant discovery that his elbows were becoming flatter. **128 pages $10**

BB-055 **"Help! A Bear is Eating Me" Mykle Hansen** - The bizarro, heart-warming, magical tale of poor planning, hubris and severe blood loss...
150 pages $11

BB-056 **"Piecemeal June" Jordan Krall** - A man falls in love with a living sex doll, but with love comes danger when her creator comes after her with crab-squid assassins. **90 pages $9**

BB-058 "The Overwhelming Urge" Andersen Prunty - A collection of bizarro tales by Andersen Prunty. **150 pages $11**

BB-059 "Adolf in Wonderland" Carlton Mellick III - A dreamlike adventure that takes a young descendant of Adolf Hitler's design and sends him down the rabbit hole into a world of imperfection and disorder. **180 pages $11**

BB-061 "Ultra Fuckers" Carlton Mellick III - Absurdist suburban horror about a couple who enter an upper middle class gated community but can't find their way out. **108 pages $9**

BB-062 "House of Houses" Kevin L. Donihe - An odd man wants to marry his house. Unfortunately, all of the houses in the world collapse at the same time in the Great House Holocaust. Now he must travel to House Heaven to find his departed fiancee. **172 pages $11**

BB-064 "Squid Pulp Blues" Jordan Krall - In these three bizarro-noir novellas, the reader is thrown into a world of murderers, drugs made from squid parts, deformed gun-toting veterans, and a mischievous apocalyptic donkey. **204 pages $12**

BB-065 "Jack and Mr. Grin" Andersen Prunty - "When Mr. Grin calls you can hear a smile in his voice. Not a warm and friendly smile, but the kind that seizes your spine in fear. You don't need to pay your phone bill to hear it. That smile is in every line of Prunty's prose." - Tom Bradley. **208 pages $12**

BB-066 "Cybernetrix" Carlton Mellick III - What would you do if your normal everyday world was slowly mutating into the video game world from Tron? **212 pages $12**

BB-072 "Zerostrata" Andersen Prunty - Hansel Nothing lives in a tree house, suffers from memory loss, has a very eccentric family, and falls in love with a woman who runs naked through the woods every night. **144 pages $11**

BB-073 **"The Egg Man" Carlton Mellick III** - It is a world where humans reproduce like insects. Children are the property of corporations, and having an enormous ten-foot brain implanted into your skull is a grotesque sexual fetish. Mellick's industrial urban dystopia is one of his darkest and grittiest to date. **184 pages $11**

BB-074 **"Shark Hunting in Paradise Garden" Cameron Pierce** - A group of strange humanoid religious fanatics travel back in time to the Garden of Eden to discover it is invested with hundreds of giant flying maneating sharks. **150 pages $10**

BB-075 **"Apeshit" Carlton Mellick III** - Friday the 13th meets Visitor Q. Six hipster teens go to a cabin in the woods inhabited by a deformed killer. An incredibly fucked-up parody of B-horror movies with a bizarro slant. **192 pages $12**

BB-076 **"Fuckers of Everything on the Crazy Shitting Planet of the Vomit At smosphere" Mykle Hansen** - Three bizarro satires. Monster Cocks, Journey to the Center of Agnes Cuddlebottom, and Crazy Shitting Planet. **228 pages $12**

BB-077 **"The Kissing Bug" Daniel Scott Buck** - In the tradition of Roald Dahl, Tim Burton, and Edward Gorey, comes this bizarro anti-war children's story about a bohemian conenose kissing bug who falls in love with a human woman. **116 pages $10**

BB-078 **"MachoPoni" Lotus Rose** - It's My Little Pony... *Bizarro* style! A long time ago Poniworld was split in two. On one side of the Jagged Line is the Pastel Kingdom, a magical land of music, parties, and positivity. On the other side of the Jagged Line is Dark Kingdom inhabited by an army of undead ponies. **148 pages $11**

BB-079 **"The Faggiest Vampire" Carlton Mellick III** - A Roald Dahl-esque children's story about two faggy vampires who partake in a mustache competition to find out which one is truly the faggiest. **104 pages $10**

BB-080 **"Sky Tongues" Gina Ranalli** - The autobiography of Sky Tongues, the biracial hermaphrodite actress with tongues for fingers. Follow her strange life story as she rises from freak to fame. **204 pages $12**

BB-081 **"Washer Mouth" Kevin L. Donihe** - A washing machine becomes human and pursues his dream of meeting his favorite soap opera star. **244 pages $11**

BB-082 **"Shatnerquake" Jeff Burk** - All of the characters ever played by William Shatner are suddenly sucked into our world. Their mission: hunt down and destroy the real William Shatner. **100 pages $10**

BB-083 **"The Cannibals of Candyland" Carlton Mellick III** - There exists a race of cannibals that are made of candy. They live in an underground world made out of candy. One man has dedicated his life to killing them all. **170 pages $11**

BB-084 **"Slub Glub in the Weird World of the Weeping Willows" Andrew Goldfarb** - The charming tale of a blue glob named Slub Glub who helps the weeping willows whose tears are flooding the earth. There are also hyenas, ghosts, and a voodoo priest **100 pages $10**

BB-085 **"Super Fetus" Adam Pepper** - Try to abort this fetus and he'll kick your ass! **104 pages $10**

BB-086 **"Fistful of Feet" Jordan Krall** - A bizarro tribute to spaghetti westerns, featuring Cthulhu-worshipping Indians, a woman with four feet, a crazed gunman who is obsessed with sucking on candy, Syphilis-ridden mutants, sexually transmitted tattoos, and a house devoted to the freakiest fetishes. **228 pages $12**

BB-087 **"Ass Goblins of Auschwitz" Cameron Pierce** - It's Monty Python meets Nazi exploitation in a surreal nightmare as can only be imagined by Bizarro author Cameron Pierce. **104 pages $10**

BB-088 **"Silent Weapons for Quiet Wars" Cody Goodfellow** - "This is high-end psychological surrealist horror meets bottom-feeding low-life crime in a techno-thrilling science fiction world full of Lovecraft and magic..." -John Skipp **212 pages $12**

BB-089 "Warrior Wolf Women of the Wasteland" Carlton Mellick III
Road Warrior Werewolves versus McDonaldland Mutants...post-apocalyptic fiction has never been quite like this. **316 pages $13**

BB-090 "Cursed" Jeremy C Shipp - The story of a group of characters who believe they are cursed and attempt to figure out who cursed them and why. A tale of stylish absurdism and suspenseful horror. **218 pages $15**

BB-091 "Super Giant Monster Time" Jeff Burk - A tribute to choose your own adventures and Godzilla movies. Will you escape the giant monsters that are rampaging the fuck out of your city and shit? Or will you join the mob of alien-controlled punk rockers causing chaos in the streets? What happens next depends on you. **188 pages $12**

BB-092 "Perfect Union" Cody Goodfellow - "Cronenberg's THE FLY on a grand scale: human/insect gene-spliced body horror, where the human hive politics are as shocking as the gore." -John Skipp. **272 pages $13**

BB-093 "Sunset with a Beard" Carlton Mellick III - 14 stories of surreal science fiction. **200 pages $12**

BB-094 "My Fake War" Andersen Prunty - The absurd tale of an unlikely soldier forced to fight a war that, quite possibly, does not exist. It's Rambo meets Waiting for Godot in this subversive satire of American values and the scope of the human imagination. **128 pages $11**

BB-095"Lost in Cat Brain Land" Cameron Pierce - Sad stories from a surreal world. A fascist mustache, the ghost of Franz Kafka, a desert inside a dead cat. Primordial entities mourn the death of their child. The desperate serve tea to mysterious creatures. A hopeless romantic falls in love with a pterodactyl. And much more. **152 pages $11**

BB-096 "The Kobold Wizard's Dildo of Enlightenment +2" Carlton Mellick III - A Dungeons and Dragons parody about a group of people who learn they are only made up characters in an AD&D campaign and must find a way to resist their nerdy teenaged players and retarded dungeon master in order to survive. 232 **pages $12**

BB-097 **"My Heart Said No, but the Camera Crew Said Yes!" Bradley Sands** - A collection of short stories that are crammed with the delightfully odd and the scurrilously silly. **140 pages $13**

BB-098 "A Hundred Horrible Sorrows of Ogner Stump" Andrew Goldfarb - Goldfarb's acclaimed comic series. A magical and weird journey into the horrors of everyday life. **164 pages $11**

BB-099 "Pickled Apocalypse of Pancake Island" Cameron Pierce
A demented fairy tale about a pickle, a pancake, and the apocalypse. **102 pages $8**

BB-100 "Slag Attack" Andersen Prunty - Slag Attack features four visceral, noir stories about the living, crawling apocalypse.A slag is what survivors are calling the slug-like maggots raining from the sky, burrowing inside people, and hollowing out their flesh and their sanity. **148 pages $11**

BB-101 "Slaughterhouse High" Robert Devereaux - A place where schools are built with secret passageways, rebellious teens get zippers installed in their mouths and genitals, and once a year, on that special night, one couple is slaughtered and the bits of their bodies are kept as souvenirs. **304 pages $13**

BB-102 "The Emerald Burrito of Oz" John Skipp & Marc Levinthal
OZ IS REAL! Magic is real! The gate is really in Kansas! And America is finally allowing Earth tourists to visit this weird-ass, mysterious land. But when Gene of Los Angeles heads off for summer vacation in the Emerald City, little does he know that a war is brewing...a war that could destroy both worlds. **280 pages $13**

BB-103 "The Vegan Revolution... with Zombies" David Agranoff
When there's no more meat in hell, the vegans will walk the earth. **160 pages $11**

BB-104 "The Flappy Parts" Kevin L Donihe - Poems about bunnies, LSD, and police abuse. You know, things that matter. 132 **pages $11**

BB-105 **"Sorry I Ruined Your Orgy" Bradley Sands** - Bizarro humorist Bradley Sands returns with one of the strangest, most hilarious collections of the year. **130 pages $11**

BB-106 **"Mr. Magic Realism" Bruce Taylor** - Like Golden Age science fiction comics written by Freud, *Mr. Magic Realism* is a strange, insightful adventure that spans the furthest reaches of the galaxy, exploring the hidden caverns in the hearts and minds of men, women, aliens, and biomechanical cats. **152 pages $11**

BB-107 **"Zombies and Shit" Carlton Mellick III** - "Battle Royale" meets "Return of the Living Dead." Mellick's bizarro tribute to the zombie genre. **308 pages $13**

BB-108 **"The Cannibal's Guide to Ethical Living" Mykle Hansen** - Over a five star French meal of fine wine, organic vegetables and human flesh, a lunatic delivers a witty, chilling, disturbingly sane argument in favor of eating the rich.. **184 pages $11**

BB-109 **"Starfish Girl" Athena Villaverde** - In a post-apocalyptic underwater dome society, a girl with a starfish growing from her head and an assassin with sea anenome hair are on the run from a gang of mutant fish men. **160 pages $11**

BB-110 **"Lick Your Neighbor" Chris Genoa** - Mutant ninjas, a talking whale, kung fu masters, maniacal pilgrims, and an alcoholic clown populate Chris Genoa's surreal, darkly comical and unnerving reimagining of the first Thanksgiving. **303 pages $13**

BB-111 **"Night of the Assholes" Kevin L. Donihe** - A plague of assholes is infecting the countryside. Normal everyday people are transforming into jerks, snobs, dicks, and douchebags. And they all have only one purpose: to make your life a living hell.. **192 pages $11**

BB-112 **"Jimmy Plush, Teddy Bear Detective" Garrett Cook** - Hardboiled cases of a private detective trapped within a teddy bear body. **180 pages $11**